TASHA BLACK STARTER LIBRARY

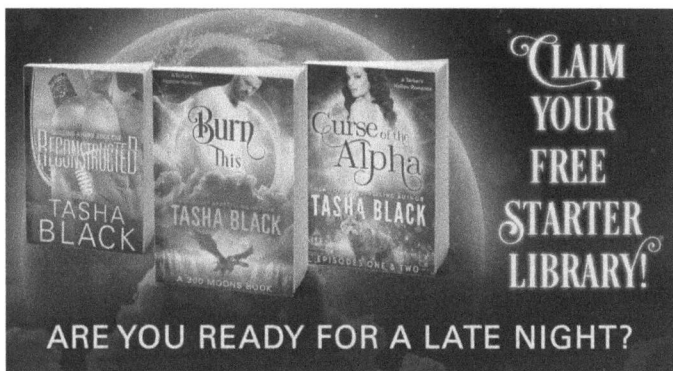

SOLO

STARGAZER ALIEN MAIL ORDER BRIDES
(BOOK 12)

TASHA BLACK

13TH STORY PRESS

13th Story Press PO Box 506 Swarthmore, PA 19081

13thStoryPress@gmail.com

SOLO

1

CECILY

C ecily breathed in the delicious air of the meadow. She knew she was dreaming, but the details seemed more real than any dream she'd ever had. Crystal drops of dew sparkled on the leaves of the ancient maples and oaks surrounding the clearing, and a low mist clung to the ground as it always had at dawn.

Cecily hadn't been in the glade since she was a child. She and her friends had played here often, pretending to be the Knights of the Round Table.

It was certainly the children's kingdom. The only other regular visitors were the Quakers in town, who used to come for their outdoor weddings. Cecily and her friends would sneak up and watch through the trees as the women in white cotton braided their long hair with ribbons and flowers, and the shirtless men danced and played their guitars under the afternoon sun. The most interesting part had always been the kiss at the end of the ceremony.

Though her mother called the Quakers hippies, Cecily herself couldn't imagine anything more romantic. It was half Shakespeare, half King Arthur.

Cecily had always imagined she would have her first kiss in the meadow.

It hadn't worked out that way, of course. Her actual first kiss had been at the town pool on a blisteringly hot day, with the scent of chlorine thick in the air. It hadn't been particularly romantic.

She'd always wanted a second chance at a first kiss in the glade.

But that could never happen. Aside from the obvious fact that her fist kiss was more than a few kisses ago, her Aunt Stacy told her the woods behind the high school had been leveled to make a parking lot for the new shopping center.

Of course, anything was possible in a dream.

She took a few steps forward. A rabbit hopped into the trees, but otherwise it was perfectly still, nothing but bird-song and the rustle of the breeze through the grass.

Cecily found that odd. There should be sounds coming from the shopping center, it couldn't be more than a couple of hundred yards away.

She closed her eyes and listened, but there was no hint of car engines or any other human interference.

The breeze caressed her hair like a lover and she opened her eyes again.

She wasn't alone anymore.

A man stood at the center of the glade. He was built like a god, tall, with broad shoulders, dark hair and piercing blue eyes.

There was something familiar about him, but she knew there had never been anyone like this in her hometown.

His hungry gaze beckoned and she went to him without hesitation.

The dewy grass tickled her bare toes as she closed the

distance between them. The air seemed to hum with electricity.

He lifted his hands, palms outward as she reached him and she placed her hands against his, knowing instinctively what he wanted from her.

The air around them swirled and out of the corner of her eye Cecily saw ghost images, like a sped-up special effect, herself and her friends as children, the weddings, the rabbits and the squirrels, the dawning and setting of a hundred translucent suns.

At first she was frightened, but the man sent waves of remembered comfort through the place where their hands touched.

And then it was something more than comfort.

The rush of memories receded as she looked up into his ocean blue eyes and lost herself to the agony of longing she saw there.

He leaned down slowly, as if afraid she would startle like one of the rabbits from her memory.

But Cecily had never craved anything more than this man's kiss.

When he pressed his mouth to hers, she saw a universe of stars spread out before her and heard the sound of distant chimes.

Flames of desire licked her insides and she kissed him back greedily, tasting the starlight of distant planets, feeling crystalline sand between her toes.

She was there and she was not there.

She was lost and found, tangled in the arms of this strange prince, in the enchanted glade of her childhood, panting with lust and yet transported beyond the confines of her body.

"Please," she whispered, not sure what she was begging for.

His mouth smiled against her lips and she felt the press of his big body more firmly against hers. For all his gentleness the evidence of his own need pulsed hard and huge between them.

He pulled away slightly to look at her.

She had the feeling again that she knew him, but his identity was just out of the reach of her lust-addled mind.

"Cecily," he said softly.

She searched his face for clues.

"Cecily," he repeated, louder this time.

The glade began to fade away.

There was a knocking sound.

"Cecily," Kate's voice said.

Cecily turned and found she was in her bed, tangled in the sheets, gray dawn filtering through the blinds.

"I'm up, I'm up," she called to her roommate.

"Awesome," Kate called back. "We've got to get on the road soon. The guys are grabbing coffee."

The guys.

She knew who the mysterious stranger was now, of course.

She couldn't escape him, even in her dreams - Solo, the tall, dark and handsome, the gentleman, the alien. He was her ceaseless companion by day and her reckless lover by night.

Well, in her dreams at least.

Though she had every intention of resisting the attraction in real life, in these moments between sleep and waking she wondered how long she could realistically hold out.

Cecily stretched and unwound the sheets from around herself.

There was no point worrying about it today. Today was the day they all piled into the rented RV and began their journey west. She wouldn't be thrown into any dangerous scenarios for the duration of the cross-country road trip. She and her two roommates, and the three aliens they had taken in, would be thrown together twenty-four seven. They wouldn't have the time, or the opportunity, for any fooling around.

It was still unbelievable to Cecily to learn that there was life on other planets, let alone that she and her roommates had taken in three fugitive aliens. When the other two women began falling in love with the massive, hunky men, Cecily had decided to steel her heart against the temptation.

She lived a wonderful, carefree life, traveling the country to do make-up and special effects. She had a community of close colleagues, no shortage of friends with benefits when she wanted them, and zero intention of pinning her hopes and emotions on a man. Her mother had allowed herself to be hogtied by love and Cecily saw where that had gotten her.

So Solo was hot, so what? Cecily could have nearly any guy she wanted. Solo's impeccable manners and kind-hearted smile could make someone else happy. Cecily was her own woman.

Though the thought of Solo and another woman did give her a pang, Cecily would get over it. She always did. She had a handful of ex-friends-with-benefits who had settled down. There had been no hurt feelings or jealousy on her part. Hell, she was "Aunt Cecily" to one or two of their kids. Solo would be no different.

Solo needed more than a fling. He needed to find a

woman to *click* with so he could become permanently
human and thereby cement peaceful relations between
Earth and his home planet, Aerie.

Maybe she could help him pick someone nice, someone
who would appreciate him.

The thought troubled her somehow, and she pushed it
aside, grabbing her robe and heading to the shower.

Hopefully, a hot shower and an even hotter cup of coffee
would tame her wild emotions.

It was going to be a fun day - she was sure of it. Cecily
had always loved road trips.

2

SOLO

Solo carefully placed the last of Beatrix's belongings on the sidewalk near the recreational vehicle Kate's agent had rented for their journey.

He paused for a moment, stretching, trying to think of any reason to stall.

He had moved all of his own and his brothers' things down, and then all of Kate's and now Bea's.

The only thing left to do was to load Cecily's things.

But Solo couldn't risk moving them.

"Is that everything?" Beatrix asked. She had been loading bottles of water and cans of soda into a cooler next to the vehicle while Solo ran up and down.

"It is nearly everything," he told her politely.

"What's left?" she asked.

"Just Cecily's things," he told her, trying not to wince. There was no way he could explain his hesitation to her, and he hoped she wouldn't ask.

"Oh," Bea said, sounding surprised.

Solo could hardly blame her. Bea had recently been

mated to his brother Buck. And Kate and Kirk were together as well.

It was hard not to imagine that everyone was looking at him and Cecily and wondering when they would bond. They were the only ones left.

For his part, Solo wanted very badly to take Cecily as his mate.

But his intended was a puzzle. She was kind and light-hearted, and yet she slipped through his fingers each time he tried to connect with her more deeply.

Solo would not rush their mating, not until he understood her through and through. And he refused to use his gift to aid their connection. It seemed like a betrayal of sorts, and that was no way to begin a relationship. Everything with Cecily must be just right, which meant Solo had to be patient and let things happen in their own time rather than use his power to provide a shortcut to a connection.

This decision made him feel content in his good manners.

But it made helping her move her things... complicated.

"Hey can you help me with this?" Cecily asked breathlessly.

He turned to see that she had come out of the lobby behind him, her arms full of even more belongings.

Spilling out of her bags were notebooks, a phone cord, and her laptop case.

He couldn't safely touch any of it.

Solo opened his mouth and closed it again.

"Here you go," Buck said from behind him, jogging up to take the bags from Cecily's hands.

Solo thanked his lucky stars.

At least his brothers understood his situation.

Kirk caught up to them, a tray of coffee in one hand, a

box of doughnuts in the other. He winked at Solo and seemed to be laughing at him.

Sure, it was easy for Kirk to laugh. He had his smiling mate warm in his bed every night. His troubles were few and he had someone to share them with.

Patience, Solo, he told himself. *Everything in its own time.*

"I think this is everything," Kate said, coming out of the lobby with an enormous stack of Beatrix's things.

Solo nearly did a double take, then he remembered that she had likely received his brother's gift when they mated. Kirk could manipulate gravity - making light things heavy or heavy things light.

Now it appeared that Kate could do it too. She looked enormously pleased with herself, though Cecily stared at her in abject wonder. If Kate had shared Kirk's gift, she hadn't told her friends about it.

Solo wondered if Cecily might share his gift when their time came to be mated.

The idea brought him no joy. His gift could just as well be called a curse. He had no wish to burden her with it.

"Are we ready?" Kate asked, sounding excited.

"Yeah," Cecily said. "I'll take the first shift driving, if you want."

"Sounds good," Kate said, tossing Cecily the keys. "Solo will sit shotgun and keep you company."

"Are there many predators?" Solo asked. He had not expected they would be traveling through dangerous territory, but he was prepared to defend their group if the need arose.

Cecily began laughing almost immediately.

Kate looked back and forth between Cecily and Solo.

"Shotgun," Cecily gasped between giggles. "You told him to sit shotgun."

"Is the shotgun seat not the position for the party member whose job is to prevent attacks by animals and outlaws?" Solo asked.

Cecily began giggling again.

Solo was not in the least embarrassed. If his failure to understand amused her, he was at her service. He loved the carefree sound of his mate's laughter.

"I guess that is the reason for the term, but we normally just mean the front passenger seat these days when we say it," Cecily explained. "We don't expect to bump into any outlaws."

"Excellent," Solo said. "But if we do, I will be prepared to protect you no matter which seat I am sitting in."

"Thank you," Cecily said sincerely.

"It is my pleasure," Solo told her slowly, enjoying the way her cheeks tinted pink before she turned away.

Kate and Bea were still giggling behind his back.

He turned and winked at them.

"Let's get this show on the road," Cecily said.

He could tell by the triumphant note of her voice that she was looking forward to their journey.

And if she had fun, so would he. Her joy already brought him joy, and they were not yet mated.

Solo slipped into the shotgun seat, armed with only the hope in his heart.

3

CECILY

Cecily had just begun to settle in and enjoy the road. Getting out of the city during her first hour of driving such an enormous vehicle for the first time had been a little hairy.

Solo seemed to know instinctively that the best thing he could do was to stay quiet and attentive. His big, silent presence was somehow comforting.

Thoughts of his big body led Cecily down a path she didn't want to explore. She fixed her gaze out the window at the cars on the highway. They looked so small from up in the RV's driver's seat.

"This is truly an efficient vehicle," Solo observed, his deep voice sending a little shiver down Cecily's spine.

"I don't know if I would call it that," she said, ruefully studying the fuel gauge. "We're going to burn through a lot of gas on this trip."

"Sorry, I didn't mean efficient as far as fuel consumption," Solo said. "I meant the efficiency of having everything you need in one place - sleeping quarters, bathing area, food storage and even games, all inside your vehicle."

"Well, no one would want to live in this thing for long, but we do have a long distance to travel," Cecily said. "It's nearly three thousand miles."

"Wow, that is an unbelievable distance," Solo said.

She heard the smile in his voice and saw that he was smirking at her.

Oh.

"Yeah, I guess you've traveled a lot further than that, huh?" she asked.

"We did," he allowed. "Designing a craft that would get us here and still accommodate the needs of our human forms was a challenge."

"But you guys were up to it," Cecily said. "That's pretty amazing."

"I helped to design that ship," Solo told her. "It was great fun to solve the puzzle of how to accommodate for waste and nourishment. Humans are very adept consumers and producers. It's tricky when there is so much time and distance involved."

"*You* designed that ship?" she asked.

"I was part of a team that designed and stocked it," he said. "They brought me in because of my work on the bio engineering."

"What bio engineering?" she asked.

"I was also part of the team that grew the human forms and piloted the technology we used for migration," he told her.

"That's... incredible," she whispered, stealing a glance at him.

He looked as relaxed and regal as usual. She never would have imagined he was a scientist, and certainly not gifted to the point where he would be able to build human bodies from scratch.

"What's incredible is the human form," he said softly, shooting her a look that made her think he might have her particular form in mind. "I've never seen anything like it. We put together a blueprint to reverse engineer a body. Then we studied the blueprint and it seemed impossible that such a design could sustain life. Even as we assembled the first form it seemed as if it couldn't function, it wouldn't be able to walk, to breathe. But... here we are."

"Here we are," she echoed, still stunned.

"It's wonderful to me, that given your fragile, hungry forms, you can accomplish any feat of engineering or art - anything at all beyond survival," Solo said. "It's triumphant and terrible at the same time."

"Hard to watch, huh?" Cecily teased.

"On the contrary," Solo purred. "It is magical to watch. I find it seductive and tragic and very, very beautiful."

Cecily felt his words as acutely as if they were his hands caressing her body. She gripped the steering wheel and prayed for deliverance.

"But we were talking about efficiency," Solo said lightly. "And this is where all the intricate engineering of the human form goes mad. Because although there is efficiency and balance in the machine that is the body, that efficiency does not translate to the actual behavior of humans."

"What do you mean?" Cecily asked.

"You are hungry and so you eat," Solo said. "So when you are no longer hungry, you stop eating, correct?"

"I guess so," Cecily said. "Unless the food is particularly delicious."

"The taste has nothing to do with the needs of the body," Solo pointed out. "Too much food can strain the system. But, yes, I learned quickly about the joys of eating certain foods. This can perhaps be labeled a minor original design flaw, too many receptors in the tongue. Not a big deal."

Cecily laughed. "I guess not."

"But what about other human inefficiencies?" Solo asked. "Drinking too much alcohol, taking chemicals that damage one's perception of reality, harming oneself, all of these can be found on Earth."

"That's true," Cecily said, feeling sad for her planetary brothers and sisters for their addictions to be on display for other worlds to notice. "But for many of these there was a design flaw, or maybe a nurturing flaw - some sadness in that particular human's past that gives them a bent for self-destruction."

"Is that what happened to you, Cecily? Was there a sadness in your life?" Solo asked.

"I-I'm not an addict," Cecily explained, horrified. "I probably drink less than most single women my age."

"I don't mean an addiction, Cecily," he said at once. "I mean that you are of age, and yet you deny yourself the pleasure and comfort of a mate."

Cecily felt her cheeks turn red. She glanced in the rear view mirror to see if the others were listening. But Buck and Bea were wearing headphones and Kate and Kirk were wrapped in each other's arms, whispering.

"I'm not denying myself anything," she said quietly. "It's just not something I want right now."

"All of the eggs you will ever have were fully formed in your ovaries before you were born," Solo said. "Prolonging your mating years could make childbearing difficult. Do you not want to rear any young?"

Cecily was at a loss for words.

"Oh no, this is a personal question, isn't it?" Solo said

suddenly. "My apologies, Cecily. It was unmannerly for me to mention it. I did not think of it until it was said."

She stole another glance at him.

He looked truly regretful.

"It's fine," she told him. "You're allowed to ask me personal questions since we're friends, though I might not always answer them. But you shouldn't ask other women that question."

"I understand," Solo said. "Thank you for permitting me the indulgence. I am glad we are friends. And of course you do not need to answer."

She smiled, glad he understood.

"Do you know what is different about this journey than the one that brought me to Earth?" he asked, neatly changing the subject for her.

"I'll bet a lot of things are different," she said, laughing.

"Yes," he agreed. "That is true. But the biggest thing I have noticed so far is that we are traveling through so many towns and villages."

Cecily looked out the window at the rooftops over the highway. Rows of houses punctuated by fluffy green treetops went on into the distance as far as she could see.

"Most of my journey to Stargazer was light-years of travel through an uninhabited void," he told her. "We've seen more in an hour than I did in all that time."

"Was it lonely?" Cecily found herself asking.

"It was," he admitted. "But I did not know it until recently."

She glanced over at him.

He studied her, his blue eyes solemn.

"So all of this seems like more fun?" she asked, indicating the cars and billboards and rooftops out the window.

"Much more fun," he agreed. "It is incredible to think

that we are at every second passing by a place that someone thinks of as their home."

"I never thought of that," Cecily said. "But you're right - we're going to pass hundreds of thousands of homes on our trip. And that includes my old home town."

"We are going to be in the place where you were born?" Solo asked.

"Yes, we're just passing by the town," Cecily said. "I don't live there anymore."

"I want to see the place where you were a child," Solo said. "Will we have time to stop there?"

"Uh, I doubt it," Cecily said. "It's nothing fancy, just a little village in the Midwest. We'll probably want to stop in Chicago instead - there are museums there and amazing architecture. You'll love it."

"No," Solo said. "I would much rather see your small Midwest town, Cecily. Let's stop there."

"Are you guys talking about stopping?" Buck called from the backseat. "I'm hungry!"

"Me too," Kate added.

"Okay, okay," Cecily said, grateful for an opportunity to stretch her legs and cool off from the conversation with Solo. "We'll look out for something good."

So much for her thought that time on the road would be a break from their growing attraction.

It seemed that no matter where they went, or how many others were with them, some private connection transported them to an intimate space anyway.

4

SOLO

Solo gazed out the window and tried to organize his thoughts.

Since arriving on this planet, and in particular since meeting Cecily, he often found himself overwhelmed with new information and new emotions.

Their intimate conversation, his lapse in good manners, her admission that they would pass through her hometown, all of it washed over him, pulling him under like a stormy ocean.

He gazed past the road and the houses beyond to the blue horizon and took a deep breath.

He had seen Kate do this when she was practicing yoga. And though Cecily laughed at her, Kate had retorted that calming breathing techniques were a valuable way to center the mind.

Solo had tried it last night, alone in the room he used to share with his brothers. And it was true, slow, careful breaths had helped him to focus. He hoped it would work now.

He took another deep breath and began.

First he packed away the worries about his rudeness. He was learning that on this lush planet, manners were nowhere near as important as they were on Aerie. Shorter lifespans led to hasty communication. His brothers had learned this quickly, but Solo was more attuned to the old ways of Aerie. It was harder for him, even though he understood it intellectually. After a few breaths, he was able to put the day's incident aside.

Next, he carefully played back Cecily's words about mating, so as not to forget them:

I'm not denying myself anything. It's just not something I want right now.

Those last two words, *right now*, were a qualifying phrase. They softened the blow of the rest of what she had said, if he understood her properly. She did not want a mate right now. But that could mean she would want one at a later time. The thought pleased him.

He took one last deep breath and let it out slowly as he allowed his mind to explore the idea of seeing the town where Cecily had grown up.

He couldn't picture it, but the idea was irresistible. He tried to imagine Cecily as a small child, Cecily playing with toys, running up and down street with a red ball, Cecily biting the end of a pencil while doing her homework at the kitchen table.

But he couldn't do it. He couldn't picture her as a child - he could only envision her shorter.

Thankfully, that wasn't the reason he wanted to see the place where she had been a nestling. The real reason was that he felt if he could experience the place where she had become who she was now, he might also understand her better. Maybe then he could learn to fill her empty spaces, be the mate she deserved.

She had denied there being a sadness in her past, but he had seen her luscious lips tighten and the slight narrowing of her eyes.

Solo wondered if he could find that wrong in her past, and right it.

"Whoa, what's *that*?" Buck cried from the back, distracting Solo from his meditation.

Solo looked out the window to see what Buck was pointing at.

A grassy field led back from the roadside to where the driveway ended at a small metal dwelling whose sign proclaimed it to be *The Dino Diner - Home of the Bronto Burger.*

The field was populated by a herd of enormous painted metal dinosaurs in various poses.

A Tyrannosaurus rex towered above the others, a ruthless expression on its face.

Just below it, a triceratops gazed placidly at the car as if to say, *That T. rex is all bark and no bite.*

"Does this place have food?" Kirk wondered from the far back seat.

"Who cares?" Bea said. "We're stopping - I need to sketch these."

Cecily laughed and pulled into the driveway.

They parked behind the Dino Diner, which was decidedly less interesting than the front.

"Food first, kids, then dinosaurs," Cecily said sternly, causing Bea and Kate to laugh.

This was odd, Cecily did seem to be the leader among the girls, but she never told them what to do.

"That's what parents always tell their children," Cecily explained to him as they walked around to the front door of the diner. "Kate and Bea and I have heard our parents say that kind of thing on every road trip we've ever been on."

"I see," Solo said.

He jogged ahead and held the door open, allowing everyone inside.

The diner was bright and fragrant. Shining metal tables with colorful tops could be found at each booth. Waitresses glided between the tables on their way to and from the steaming kitchen he could just glimpse over the counter. It was a tiny universe of activity.

A waitress approached them.

"Thanks for coming to the Dino Diner," she said with a big smile. "Follow me."

They followed her to a large booth in the corner overlooking the dinosaur field.

Kate, Bea and Cecily slid into the side with its back to the field.

Kirk, Buck and Solo sat opposite them. It wasn't until he was seated that Solo realized how naturally they had all paired off, his brothers gazing at their mates, and he at his intended. The prehistoric view was wasted on Solo, since he only had eyes for Cecily.

The waitress leaned on the table, inadvertently showing the tops of her breasts between the unfastened top buttons of her blouse.

Solo looked up into her eyes politely so as not to rest his gaze on her bosom. He had been told it was very impolite to do otherwise.

"My name is Amber and I'll be taking care of you today," the waitress said with a big smile. "Here at the Dino Diner, we're known for the Bronto Burger - two fresh patties topped with lettuce, tomatoes and our special Tricero-sauce."

"Is it made with real brontosaurus?" Buck asked in wonder.

Bea kicked his leg under the table.

"Sorry about him," she told the waitress. "Please go on."

"Our special today is the Jurassic Pork," Amber went on gamely. "That's sweet barbecued pulled pork on a potato roll served with chips and slaw. Or you can substitute Broccoli-o-saurus Bites for just three dollars more."

"Paying three dollars to get bitten by something hardly seems fair," Kirk muttered.

"Can't take these jokers anywhere," Cecily said brightly. "We'll take six specials and six cokes, please."

"Six Jurassic Porks and six cokes," the waitress said.

"And no bites," Kirk said. "Please."

Kate kicked him under the table.

"Ouch. You kicked me."

The waitress disappeared into the kitchen.

"Okay," Cecily said giggling. "The dinosaur stuff is just pretend. It's a gimmick. None of the food really has anything to do with dinosaurs."

"What's a gimmick?" Solo asked.

Cecily tilted her head to the side to think, sending her curls spilling over one shoulder in way that made him forget his question.

"I guess I'd say it's like a trick," she said.

"Something to get your attention while someone is trying to sell you something," Kate added.

"Like the leprechaun that sells cereal," Kirk said wisely.

"Yes, like that," Cecily agreed. "The dinosaurs are just for fun, to get your attention when you're driving past the place."

"It worked," Buck said.

Solo looked down at the menu. Nearly everything on it

was named for a dinosaur. "So none of these creatures exist anymore?" he asked.

Cecily shook her head and frowned. "They are all extinct."

"But they were not killed off by humans," he pointed out, hoping to cheer her up.

"Most of them weren't," she agreed. She slid her hand across the table to tap on one of the menu items.

His hand was dangerously close to hers.

Solo resisted the impulse to grab her hand, instead pulling his back. He couldn't be too careful.

"The dodo is extinct because of man's interference," Cecily said. "It was hunted by sailors and its habitat was destroyed."

"Six cokes," Amber said, placing the drinks in front of them with a wide smile. "I'll be back in a jiffy with your lunch."

Solo watched her sail off between the tables.

A group of young women a few tables over stopped their giggling and stared at him.

When he turned back to Cecily he could hear them giggling again.

"Looks like someone's got himself a fan club," Bea said. "Ha."

Cecily's eyes narrowed slightly, then she smiled.

"What do you mean?" Solo asked Bea. He knew what a fan was. They had spent plenty of time dealing with them at the comic cons. But he didn't expect any of the girls to have a club of fans that met in a restaurant with a dinosaur gimmick.

"Oh nothing, I was only kidding," Bea said, glancing at Cecily.

Before long, Amber came back with two heaping trays of

food and for a while there was no talking at all as the group handed out their meals and dug in.

Solo was fascinated by the endless variety in human foodstuffs. He liked this meal very much, though he would have liked to have cooked it himself. He enjoyed the scientific aspect of portioning things out and mixing them together to create his own meals. Unfortunately that wasn't something the women seemed to do very often. He wondered if preparing one's own food was expensive.

Cecily smiled at him from across the table. She had a small smudge of barbecue sauce in the corner of her mouth and he longed to kiss it away.

"I have sauce on my face, don't I?" she asked.

He nodded and pointed to the corner of his own mouth to show her.

She swiped the wrong side with her napkin, then raised her eyebrows at him in question.

"No, the other side," he said, smiling.

She tried again, still missed the spot.

"Can you...?" she asked him, leaning forward.

Solo's heart raced as two instincts pulled him in opposite directions. One demanded that he touch her. The other feared what he might learn if he did.

He grabbed a napkin and very gently and carefully removed the sauce without his skin brushing hers.

Usually he could touch people and things and nothing happened. But with Cecily he feared that his emotions would turn it into something different.

"Thanks," she said, her dimples appearing.

"Okay, lovebirds," Bea teased. "I think it's time to hit the road if we want to make it to the hotel by check-in."

"We're not staying in the RV?" Buck asked her as they all slipped out of the booth.

"The RV is okay in a pinch," Kate explained. "But a hotel is more comfortable."

They were in line to pay their bill when the table of giggling women got in line behind them.

"Hi there," one of the women said to Solo.

"Hello," he replied politely, wondering why she was looking him up and down so thoroughly. He hoped what he was wearing was proper attire for the diner.

"You know what, I'm going to run to the bathroom," Kate said, handing Kirk her bag.

"Me too," Cecily said, holding her bag out to Solo.

He hesitated. There was probably nothing on the bag that he could touch and trigger anything, but...

Buck grabbed Cecily's bag from her. "I'll hold that for you," he said.

She frowned and headed off after Bea.

When the bill was paid, the other four went outside to explore the dinosaurs.

They were incredible, though up close Solo could see that their paint was flaking in places and a bit of rust showed through here and there.

Bea pulled out her sketchpad and began to draw, her hands moving quickly.

Buck leaned on a dinosaur behind her, looking over her shoulder as she worked.

"It's interesting, isn't it, brother?" Kirk asked. "That humans are half in love with a species that didn't live in their own time?"

"They are fascinating creatures, humans," Solo nodded.

"*We* are fascinating creatures," Kirk corrected him.

Solo nodded, though it wasn't entirely true. At least not for himself yet. Kirk had *clicked* permanently into his human body the moment of his mating with Kate, as Buck had with Bea.

But Solo was still free to slip the bonds of this flesh if he were sent back to Aerie.

He was determined not to do so. After living in the sensory excess of this marvelous planet, he wanted to stay.

And more importantly, he was bonded to Cecily whether she reciprocated his feelings or not. He could no longer imagine life without her.

"Are you guys ready?" Kate called to them.

Cecily did not look at Solo as she walked quickly past.

"Sure," Kirk said. He strode up to Kate and wrapped an arm around her.

She looked up at him with shining eyes, as if she had missed him horribly during their few minutes apart.

Cecily was already entering the RV, right behind Bea and Buck.

"I'll take the next shift driving," Kate said.

Cecily tossed Kate the keys and climbed into the back.

Solo followed her in, already dreaming about how nice it would be to share a seat with her. They would gaze out the window together and talk. And though he would not touch her, her closeness would enfold him in the euphoria he felt each time she was near.

5

CECILY

Cecily marched into the back of the RV and sat in the only single seat. She pulled her datebook out of her bag and pretended to study it so as to avoid making eye contact with Solo when he got in.

She knew she was being ridiculous. She didn't even want a relationship.

But Solo refusing to hold her bag for her in front of those flirting women had really hurt her feelings.

For all the puppy dog eyes he was giving her, he really didn't care if it was her he bonded with or some random floozy in a dinosaur diner. He was just another dumb, horny guy, whether he could reverse engineer a human body or not.

Maybe it was for the best that she take a step back and remember that. They had become close, but if her jealous feelings were any indication, Cecily had let things go too far. They were more than friends, whether they had ever touched or not.

Solo sat on the double seat opposite her. He had

scrunched his big body all the way to one side, as if to demonstrate that there was room for her beside him.

He caught her in his blue-eyed gaze and for a moment she was tempted to smile or to say something.

But she was kidding herself if she thought that would go anywhere good.

Instead, she buried her nose in her planner again, trying not to notice the look of dismay on his handsome face.

Kate turned the key in the ignition and the RV shuddered for a moment, then rumbled to a start.

Kirk crowed victoriously, as if they were taking off on horseback and Kate laughed with him.

Buck tucked his arm around Bea in the double seat they shared while Bea hunched over her notebook, sketching furiously, as if she hadn't noticed that she'd been plucked out of the field and into the vehicle.

Cecily only wished she had her friend's focus. She stared at the planner until the words began to blur in front of her eyes.

The datebook was always brimming with upcoming adventures, and that was how she liked it. Another day, another week, another month, another wild scheme. From monster make-up to CG effects, Cecily fed at a smorgasbord of creative opportunity - no two days in her world were the same and that was what she adored about her career.

There was certainly no room in it for settling down with silly men.

She looked out the window as the scenery streamed past and tried not to think about it Solo's way, tried not to dwell on how each rooftop was the home and shelter for a family, the likes of which she would never have.

But it was no use - he'd gotten into her head.

He'd even made her curious about seeing her own hometown again.

She thought idly about the old glade. After her dream it almost seemed possible that it was still there.

Determined to push the thoughts aside, she snagged her e-reader out of her bag and clicked on a favorite book.

RVs, hotel rooms, and hometowns aside, she always felt at home in a book.

6

SOLO

Solo climbed out of the RV and stretched his legs.

They had only been driving for an hour or two but it felt like an eternity with Cecily's nose in a book and Solo alone with nothing but his thoughts and the sights and sounds of his brothers happily in love. He'd had to content himself with reading an old driver's manual he'd found under one of the seats in the RV.

He expected they would all pair off to get coffee together, but instead Cecily marched off for the restroom, Bea and Kate in tow.

Solo sighed and headed toward a picnic table under the shade of a large tree. He leaned against the trunk to think.

Kirk and Buck approached him.

"Are you okay?" Kirk asked without preamble.

"I'm fine," Solo said.

"So polite," Buck teased. "What happened with you and Cecily?"

"I'm not sure," Solo admitted. "She was angry at me from the minute she left the bathroom back at the diner."

"Maybe Kate can tell me what's wrong," Kirk said.

"No," Solo said. "I don't think Cecily would like her friends to inform on her feelings."

"That is a wise thought," Buck said, eyebrows lifted in admiration. "You are becoming more skilled at understanding humans."

"Unfortunately, the only one I want to understand doesn't want to be mated," Solo said.

"How do you know?" Buck asked.

"She told me," Solo said. "And she meant it. I can feel it."

Buck sighed.

"Maybe we can find someone else," Kirk offered carefully. "Someone who is ready to be your mate."

"How would you have felt if I'd said that to you a few days ago about Kate?" Solo asked.

Kirk frowned and nodded. "Then you will have to bring her around."

"Why doesn't she want to be mated?" Buck asked.

"I'm not really sure," Solo said. "She's more complicated than a bio-ship's engineering manual."

"This is because you expect everything about her to be logical and orderly," Buck said. "But her feelings don't have to make sense from the outside."

"Then how am I supposed to understand?" Solo asked.

"You must try to understand her feelings from the inside," Buck said. "Learn more about her life and her past, and maybe you will learn why she is attracted to you but won't act on it."

"How can I do that?" Solo asked.

"Well, for the rest of us, the only answer would be to ask a lot of impertinent questions," Kirk said. "But for you, you would just have to—"

"—I won't do it," Solo said.

"You love her, don't you brother?" Buck asked.

Solo nodded.

"If you love her and you want to know her better, I think it might help to use your gift," Kirk said. "Just a little."

"It doesn't work the way you think," Solo said. "I can't just touch her and watch her life unfold like I'm watching a movie. And besides, it's an invasion of her privacy. It's like stealing."

"Well then, brother, you have three options," Buck said.

"Not this again." Kirk rolled his eyes.

"Flowers, jealousy, and space," Buck counted off on his fingers. "Kirk gave Kate space and she came around. I made Bea jealous..."

"You *tried* to make her jealous," Kirk put in.

"Yes, I did," Buck said. "Or you could bring her flowers and chocolates, win her over with sweetness."

"I don't think any of those things will work," Solo said sadly.

"It can't hurt to try," Buck said. "You can use some of our emergency money to buy them - maybe they have flowers or chocolate in the shops inside."

Solo shrugged. He had no better ideas, and if flowers or treats made Cecily smile they couldn't hurt his cause. Maybe he would give them a shot.

"We'll see you inside, brother," Kirk said.

Solo nodded.

He jogged back to the RV, climbed in quickly and grabbed Kirk's navy blue backpack from beside the table.

A shiny silver star hung from the zipper. He'd never noticed that before.

Without thinking, Solo took hold of it.

He had just enough time to realize he had grabbed the wrong backpack.

Then the vision lowered its ghostly curtain around him.
It was too late to stop it.

A SMALL GIRL lay on her belly in bed. Her face was hidden in
her pillow, but Solo could see the curls on her head.

Cecily.

An unknown, but somehow familiar woman sat on the
edge of the bed.

I know Father's Day is hard, the woman said.

I don't want to talk about it, the girl sniffed.

*Uncle Ray is coming to the Father's Day breakfast with you
tomorrow*, the woman said. *He's excited to be your guest at
school.*

I want a daddy, the girl said quietly.

The mother bit her lip.

I at least want to know who he is, the girl continued. *Why
won't you tell me his name?*

Because it doesn't matter, the mother said. *He's not really
your father. He's just a man. You and I are a family.*

I need to know, the girl sobbed.

Solo watched as the mother slid something out of her
pocket.

I was going to keep this until tomorrow, she said. *But I want
you to have it now.*

What?

Just a little present.

The girl sat up and Solo was surprised to see how much
little Cecily looked like her grown-up self. She had the same
constellation of freckles across her nose.

Her mother smiled and held out something that shim-
mered in the lamplight. It was a charm bracelet with a
sparkling silver star.

Little Cecily took it and read the inscription on the shiny pendant out loud, *We Are Enough.*

We are enough, Cecily, her mom said. *Always remember that. Some kids have to share their mother's love with a father or siblings. But you are my everything, my star, Cecily Page. And I will love you forever.*

Cecily smiled slowly.

Suddenly she flung her arms around her mother's neck. *Can we make hot chocolate?*

I don't see why not, her mother said with a smile.

Cecily slid the bracelet onto her wrist.

SOLO WATCHED INTENTLY but the vision was already fraying at the edges, fading into nothing.

He managed to drop the backpack where he'd found it.

He sank into a seat, deep in thought.

Cecily did not know who her father was. He wasn't part of her life, part of her family.

Solo had read Cecily's memoir, *Make-Up Sex*. The references to her many romantic conquests unfailingly made him wild with jealousy even though she was careful not to name names. But the book was mostly an interesting story of what it was like to be a make-up and special effects artist. Solo had noticed that although Cecily mentioned a variety of subjects in it, she did not mention her family, except for one reference to her mother's death.

Now she had no mother. And she had never known her father.

And she wanted - *needed* to know who he was.

Could the disappearance of her mother's mate be the reason Cecily didn't want one of her own?

An incredible idea began to occur to Solo.

If he could help Cecily to locate her father, perhaps he could give her closure. Maybe it would be enough to allow her to move on.

Solo knew that if he found her father, the man would be overjoyed. Anyone would be proud to have a daughter as accomplished as Cecily.

If Solo could give Cecily back a family, maybe she would even feel ready to begin a family of her own.

Solo forgot about the flowers and chocolate and began to formulate a real plan.

Maybe reading that driver's manual hadn't been a total waste of time after all.

7

CECILY

C ecily sat in the cafe at the truck stop, using a spoon to eat the whipped cream off the top of her frozen cappuccino.

Bea and Kate sat on the opposite side of the table, earnest expressions on their faces.

"I'm fine, guys, really," she said.

"You're not fine," Kate said. "And we're your friends - we're supposed to help you."

"No offense, but I kind of know what your advice is going to be," Cecily said. "And I'm glad for you guys, I really am. I can see how happy you are with them, but marrying an alien is not for me."

A woman at the next table looked over at them in a scandalized way.

"Figure of speech," Bea said to the woman.

The woman turned back to her own coffee.

"Listen, we are one hundred percent behind you, whether things work out with you and Solo or not," Kate said.

Cecily looked into her friend's brown eyes. She could see

that Kate was telling the truth. Their friendship would survive this.

"Thanks," she said.

"Obviously we're hoping things *do* work out with you guys," Kate added.

"He's clearly really into you," Bea said.

"I've had plenty of guys into me before," Cecily said. "I literally wrote a book about it. But where are they now?"

The other two didn't answer right away.

Cecily stabbed a straw into her drink.

"Besides, he wouldn't even hold my stuff in front of those other women," she said. "He likes me until there's someone else to preen in front of."

"I don't think that's what happened," Bea said.

"Then what did happen?" Cecily asked.

"I'm not really sure," Bea said. "But I know he isn't into impressing other women. He cares about you. He told Buck he loves you."

The thought gave Cecily pleasure, even though she didn't want it to. She tamped it down as best she could.

"No matter what they *say*, they all leave," Cecily said. "They burn out fast or they fade away. Guys are not a permanent fixture."

"Don't take this the wrong way," Kate said. "But have you ever stayed in one place long enough for a guy to have a chance to stick around?"

Cecily sighed. Her friend had a point.

"Just think about it," Kate said.

8

CECILY

Cecily stood with her friends in the lobby of a small roadside zoo. She was holding a small paper tray of fruit cups and a tiny baby bottle and wondering what she was doing with her life.

The lobby smelled like urine and sounded like a baby shower, with grown adults squealing over the kitschy items for sale.

They'd been on the road, making pretty good time, until Bea had spotted this place and swerved into the parking lot like a stunt driver for an action movie - all screeching brakes and spraying gravel. Cecily swore the RV had been balanced on two wheels at one point.

"I can't believe this, can you?" Bea asked Cecily excitedly for about the tenth time.

"It is unbelievable," Cecily assured her.

Bea didn't notice her sarcasm. She was too excited about examining the tiny food containers and wondering to Buck about what kind of animals she would be feeding them to.

Cecily gazed down at the small plastic cups of fruity stuff in her own hands. Somehow, not knowing anything about the creatures that would be eating the food made the whole thing feel even more sinister.

"Do you like animals?" Solo asked.

"I like cats and dogs," she said. "You know, normal pet animals."

"Was that a snake on the sign for this place?" Solo asked.

He sounded genuinely interested.

"Yes," Cecily said. "It was definitely a snake."

The line in the lobby began to move toward an unremarkable door in the wall. It looked like it should lead to a janitor's closet. Instead it opened into a narrow hallway.

On either side, so close she could have reached out her hands and touched both at once, were plexiglass cases holding an assortment of large snakes.

Cecily shuddered and kept her eyes on the back of the person in front of her.

She tried not to listen to the guide ahead explaining that Shirleen, the proprietor of the zoo, had built all the exhibits herself. If Cecily thought too hard about that, she might start to worry about how much Shirleen knew about zoo safety and snake containment. And that way madness lay.

"They are very beautiful," Solo said. "But how are we supposed to give them their snacks?"

"Um, I don't think these snacks are for them," Cecily said. "Snakes are meat eaters. And most of them prefer live prey."

There were delighted squeals from the front of the group as the hallway opened up into a larger room.

"Now what?" Cecily grumbled, expecting to be greeted by some new, scaly thing.

But there was only a man holding a bunny. It sat calmly in his arms and accepted the patting and adoration of the group with quiet dignity.

Cecily longed to stroke those velvet ears.

"I don't care what it eats, I want to pet it," Solo announced.

Cecily laughed and approached with him.

The bunny submitted to their attentions with a cool indifference that was spoiled only by the endearing wiggling of his nose.

Solo's hand grazed hers and she felt that zap of electricity between them that she'd felt at every accidental touch since they met.

They moved on down another hallway.

The person in front of Cecily stopped walking suddenly and she barely managed to avoid smashing into them.

Solo bumped into her, but caught her by the shoulders so she was in no danger of falling.

"I'm very sorry," he said.

"No worries," she said. "I think my backpack took the impact."

She laughed, knowing her backpack was overstuffed. She always carried an extra sweatshirt, along and a few other necessities.

"Hey, what's that on the zipper?" Solo asked, indicating the small silver star that dangled there.

"Oh, it's just something my mom gave me," she said. "It used to be a bracelet, but I outgrew it a long time ago."

"I read your book," Solo said carefully. "I'm sorry your mom died."

Cecily swallowed over the lump that was suddenly in her throat. She'd thought she was past the sudden tears that used to prickle her eyelids. But Solo's sincere and simple words had broken something open in her again.

"Do you have lots of mementos from her?" he asked as they passed yet another reptile cage.

"Not really," Cecily said. "I travel a lot, so I can't bring that kind of stuff with me."

"Do you keep other things from your childhood that remind you of her?" Solo asked.

Cecily shook her head.

"Oh," he said. "Does it make you feel sad that all your things are gone?"

"I'm not super sentimental," Cecily said, shrugging. She didn't like talking about the past, her mom, or any of the things that made her sad.

Solo nodded, but he looked troubled.

It hit her that he had just left everyone and everything he had ever known behind on Aerie.

"All of my stuff isn't really gone," she told him. "I have a storage locker back in Englewood."

"Is that where you live when you aren't traveling?" Solo asked.

"No, that's my hometown," she said. "When my mom died I went back to clean out the house so it could be sold. I got rid of almost everything, but I put a bunch of personal stuff in storage to worry about later."

"When will you attend to it?" Solo asked.

"I don't know," Cecily shook her head. "The storage fee is cheap and I never really made a plan. I guess maybe I'll leave it there forever."

She tried to laugh, but it came out more like a sigh. The whole thing just made her sad.

But it was nice that Solo was curious.

They came up to another set of plexiglass cases. A small monkey hopped up and down on a square of wood, pointing at something in the wall.

A little girl ahead of them was waving back at the monkey.

"That monkey wants something," Solo said.

They watched it for a moment. It pointed up at the wall, then pressed its little hand against its face.

"Oh," Cecily said, realizing. "Look at that."

A PVC pipe stuck out of the wall, the other end was just above the monkey's little platform.

"Ah," said Solo.

He approached the little girl.

"Excuse me," he said politely. "I think the monkey wants you to put food in the pipe for him."

The girl looked at the pipe in the wall, the monkey and Solo, her eyes dancing in delight.

The monkey jumped up and down, shoving imaginary food into its little mouth.

The girl snatched a cup of fruit from her tray and moved to dump it down the pipe. But in her excitement she spilled it and most of it fell into a floor grate.

"Oh no," she cried.

Solo plucked the fruit cup off his own paper tray and handed it to her at once.

"Thank you," she said.

"Madison," her mother said reprovingly.

"It's okay," Solo said.

The mom looked him up and down appreciatively.

Cecily felt jealousy bubbling up.

But Solo had eyes only for the child, and the monkey, both of whom seemed positively giddy with anticipation.

The girl stood on her tiptoes to slide the fruit into the pipe and they all stepped back to watch as the monkey enthusiastically shoveled fruit into his mouth.

"Yes," Madison cried, offering Solo a high five.

"Excellent," he said, smacking her hand back lightly.

"Thank you," the mother mouthed to him.

He smiled and shook his head, then moved back to Cecily.

"That was nice," she said.

"Yes, I'm glad the monkey was pleased," he replied.

"No, I meant it was nice of you to help the little girl," she said.

"I like helping people," he said.

"Want to help me feed the monkey?" Cecily asked, offering him her fruit cup.

He laughed.

For a moment she let herself enjoy the way the sound made her insides melt, the brilliant blue of his mirth-crinkled eyes, and the way his dark hair brushed his forehead, as if even it couldn't resist the desire to caress him.

9
___

SOLO

Solo leaned against the wall and watched Cecily use the baby bottle to feed a small pig.

Though she had hesitated about nearly every animal interaction in this place, the moment she saw the piglets Cecily's eyes lit up and she dashed over to feed them.

Solo would have liked to feed a small pig himself, but it was even more pleasant to watch Cecily do it, so he gave her his bottle as well.

She leaned over the barricade and crooned to the piglet, who looked up at her intently as he drank.

And who could blame him?

Solo was looking at her intently, too.

Cecily was radiant. She smiled and the sunlight brought out the touch of auburn in her curls. As far as he was concerned she was more beautiful than any actress in any movie.

Things were better between them. He wasn't sure why, but he was glad.

"Time to go," Kate said as she walked past. "I'm going to find Bea and Buck."

Kate and Kirk had been pouring cup after cup of treats down a tube to a black bear, which sat at the bottom, solemnly slurping the morsels as they arrived.

Bea and Buck were still inside with the monkey.

"That was really fun," Cecily admitted, heading toward him with a big smile and two empty baby bottles.

"It was," he agreed, smiling down at her.

They walked slowly out to the parking lot, where the setting sun painted the sky behind the RV a vivid pink.

Cecily yawned.

"I'll drive again," Bea offered as she and the others approached.

"Awesome," Kate said. "We're a bit behind schedule because of the stop, but we should be able to make it up on the highway."

"No sweat," Bea said. "I'll make up the time."

"Carefully," Kate said.

"Yeah, of course," Bea agreed.

They all climbed in. Cecily sat beside Solo on one of the double seats.

A moment later the engine rumbled and they were back on the road.

Cecily yawned again and gazed out the window, then leaned back, casually resting herself against Solo.

Solo held his breath, marveling at the soft heat of her body against his.

None of her memories invaded. He was aware only of the soft sweet warmth of her body.

After a moment, he wrapped an arm around her and leaned back against his seat.

The RV bumped and bustled along on its journey as Bea and Buck talked quietly in the front seat. Kate and Kirk pored over a magazine together.

And Solo tried to memorize the fragrance of Cecily's hair, the sweet weight of her head against his chest.

Though his body hummed with lust, it was the honeyed ache of his heart that kept him from sleeping.

10

CECILY

ecily awoke with Solo's arms around her.
It was dark already and the others were whispering.

"Hey sleepyhead," Kate murmured to her.

"Are we there?" Cecily asked.

"Yeah, we made it," Kate said. "But we're a little later than we planned because *somebody* had to stop at that zoo."

"I regret nothing," Bea called back from the driver's seat where she was gathering her stuff.

"It was fun," Kate admitted. "Anyway, I just ran in to get the keys to our rooms but they already gave one to someone else. Are you two okay sharing a room?"

"Uh, sure," Cecily said. "That's fine."

In truth her heart was pounding with an anticipation she didn't want to deliver on.

It's just a room. Keep your head in the game. You're not getting together with him.

But she wasn't sure she could resist. Even now the thought of extricating herself from his arms just to get out of the RV was all but impossible.

Kate winked at her, dropped a key in her hand, and jogged back to grab her own stuff.

Cecily sighed.

Solo's arms loosened.

"You're tired, why don't you go relax, I'll carry our stuff," he said.

"That's okay, I can carry my own stuff," she said.

But he grabbed her backpack and both of their suitcases anyway.

She climbed out and checked the number on the key.

The motel was really a series of little cottages. They followed the directional signs to #7. It was a small white clapboard thing, set back under the pine trees. It looked suspiciously romantic.

Cecily strode up to the front door and slipped the key into the lock. The door opened into a simple room with a table and chairs, a bureau and a queen sized bed.

"One bed," Cecily said out loud before she could stop herself.

"I'll sleep in the chair," Solo told her as he entered, placing their bags on the top of the bureau.

They studied the small wooden chair.

"We can share the bed," she said. "No funny business, though."

"What is funny business?" Solo asked, sounding mystified.

"Never mind," Cecily said. "I'm going to take a shower, ok?"

"Okay," he echoed. "I'll unpack."

Under the warm water of the shower, Cecily promised herself that she would crawl into that bed and go right to sleep.

As she smoothed lotion onto her legs after the shower,

she reminded herself why it didn't make sense to get into a relationship.

While she pulled on her most modest pajamas, a silky tank top and shorts that she noticed were not very modest after all, Cecily focused her thoughts on how much she enjoyed her career, which kept her on the road at least ten months out of the year. It was not a good career for a person who wanted a relationship. And she didn't want a relationship.

She left the bathroom to find Solo had unpacked his things and set her backpack on the table. The bedside lamp gave the room a gentle glow.

"I think I'll take a shower too," he said, grabbing his stuff and heading to the bathroom.

Cecily organized her things and laid out an outfit for the next day. She plugged in her phone.

She tried not to listen to the shower water, or to picture Solo's big body, lathered with soap.

A few minutes later he emerged and she caught her breath.

He was naked but for a towel slung around his hips. A few drops of water trailed down his chest and abs.

There were no words to describe the perfection of his body or the ice blue of his eyes that seemed to be melting into an ocean of need as he gazed at her.

Cecily had fought this attraction, fought it with everything she had.

But this was too much. It was all too much. She was only human.

As she stood staring at him, he began to move toward her like a big cat on the prowl.

Cecily was struck by the restrained energy that seemed to coil through his muscular body.

He moved slowly, the tiger giving the gazelle time to flee.

But Cecily didn't want to flee, couldn't have moved even if she did. She was caught in a field of energy that seemed to surround him, mesmerized by the heat of his gaze.

She was ready to be devoured.

"Cecily," he said carefully, when he was a golden inch away from touching her.

There was power in the growl of his voice, but she wasn't afraid.

Cecily tilted her chin up to accept his kiss.

11

SOLO

S olo gazed into Cecily's eyes, indulging himself with a single instant of anticipation.

Then he bent to press his lips to hers, sealing their unspoken bargain at last.

She moaned softly and he smiled against her mouth.

He had designed this body, selected it specifically for himself. It was long, lean and well-muscled - an efficient machine for life on this planet, and sculpted to appeal to the aesthetic tastes of any human female lucky enough to come across it.

If it pleased her, Solo was proud of a job well done.

She shivered with desire in his arms.

A corresponding wave of lust was nearly his undoing. This was a dangerous game he played. It would require iron control.

He cupped her cheek and deepened their kiss.

Cecily kissed him back passionately.

Solo slid his hand down from her cheek to caress her hair, her back.

Cecily pressed closer to him and he felt her breasts

through the thin fabric of her shirt. The sensation was incredible. He could feel the soft warmth as they flattened against his own chest, her stiff nipples the only bit that didn't mold itself to him.

He slid both hands under her bottom and lifted her up.

Cecily made a small surprised sound but didn't break their kiss. Instead she twined her arms around his neck and locked her ankles at the small of his back.

He climbed into the bed with her, pinning her to the mattress with his hips.

Cecily stroked his shoulders and slid her hands into his hair as he devoured her mouth.

His cock raged against the confines of the towel. Solo pulled away from the kiss to gather himself.

Cecily gazed up at him, her eyes soft with lust, her lips swollen.

He leaned down again and brushed her collarbone with one feather-light kiss, and another.

Her nipples strained against the fabric of her shirt.

He nuzzled one and then the other.

Cecily gasped.

Solo slid one hand under her shirt, lifting it up to reveal her beautiful breasts. He lowered his head to lick one nipple into his mouth.

It pouted against his tongue and he sucked lightly.

Cecily caught her breath.

He kissed his way to her other breast, toying with the first with his hand as he licked and sucked.

Cecily's hands clenched the sheets and he felt her hips lift against his.

He hoped he could satiate her hunger.

She wasn't ready for them to belong to each other. No matter what she told him now, it would only be her need talking. But he hoped that if he could pleasure her without *clicking* with her, it might strengthen the bond they already shared.

He tucked his fingers into her silky waistband and she lifted her bottom to help him slide her shorts and panties off.

He kissed his way down her belly and nudged her thighs apart.

She spread them willingly for him, and his heart surged with gratitude.

Though he had watched many films at the lab that were designed to stimulate his sexual organs, they were nothing but a shadow, a meager appetizer compared to the sensual feast before him.

Cecily's sex was pink as a shell and glistening, the heat and delicate fragrance that clung to her irresistible.

And this wasn't a strange woman on a flickering screen. This was Cecily, his Cecily, the brave and funny woman he adored, real and warm, allowing him to see her and touch her in this way.

Solo took a breath and begged himself to go slowly and draw out the moment for as long as possible.

He lowered his mouth and tasted her.

Cecily cried out helplessly.

Unable to restrain himself, Solo responded with what he knew she wanted, long, deep strokes of his tongue.

Cecily tangled her hands in his hair, her hips trembling.

He slid one finger against her opening and pressed it inside slowly, reveling in the velvety heat that enveloped it.

His cock pounded against the mattress.

By the three moons of Aerie, give me strength.

Cecily whimpered and lifted her hips against his mouth.

He licked around his finger, searching, and found what he was looking for.

Cecily cried out as he applied his efforts to the stiff little bud that seemed to swell and pout against his tongue.

He slid his finger slowly in and out of her delicious heat and teased and tormented her swollen clitoris until she was panting and her hands clutched in his hair.

"Please," she whispered.

The word cut through him and he gave her the quick, firm strokes she craved.

He could feel the exact moment when her ecstasy overtook her. She stilled beneath him then clasped around his finger in a series of fluttering contractions, her clit stiff against his tongue as she cried out her pleasure.

When she had stilled, he crawled up beside her.

Cecily's cheeks were pink and her eyes shiny. She looked both relaxed and surprised.

"Wow," she whispered.

"Wow," he agreed, kissing the constellation of freckles on her nose.

She turned over onto her side to face him, sending her breasts bouncing against his chest in a very pleasant way.

But when she slid her hand down his body, he caught her by the wrist.

"No," he told her.

She looked up at him in surprise.

"It's not that I don't want it," he told her.

"Clearly," she said, raising an eyebrow at the shape of him, stark and stiff against her through the towel.

"You know what happens if I *click* with you, right?" he asked.

"But you don't do that unless you're mating for life," she said, looking a little worried.

"That's right," he told her. "I would not want to do that unless we were ready to take that step. But my heart has already chosen you as my mate. So if I make love with you I'm not sure if I can stop it from happening."

"We don't have to make love," she suggested, taking his hand and rubbing his index finger across her plush lips.

He felt it in his cock and closed his eyes against the pleasure.

"No," he told her. "But I don't want to risk doing anything you're not ready for."

"That doesn't seem fair," she said. But he could feel her relaxing into the idea.

"May I hold you while we sleep?" he asked.

"Sure," she said. And in spite of all that had just passed between them, she sounded a little embarrassed.

He lay on his back and opened his arms to her.

Cecily scooted close and rested her head on his chest.

"What did you mean when you said your heart had already chosen me?" she asked after a moment. "Does that mean that all of this is inevitable? That I don't have a choice?"

"Of course you have a choice," he told her. "I have to choose you as my mate. Then you have to choose to accept me as yours. After that, we could *click*. But only if you accept me. If you asked me to leave today, I would never love another, but I would be able to go. If we clicked, I'm not sure what would happen if you didn't want me around anymore."

"Oh," she said.

"Are you sorry that I chose you?" he asked, trying not to wrap up his hopes too much in her answer.

"No," she said. "I- I really care about you, Solo. I've tried hard not to, but I can't seem to help it."

He laughed.

"I guess that's not a very romantic thing to say," she said, laughing a little.

"It's honest, and that's one of the reasons I love you," he told her, kissing the top of her head. "I'm glad you care about me."

"Me too," she said.

She was quiet a long time.

He stroked her back with his fingers.

When he was sure she must be asleep he felt her lips move against his chest.

"Let's try, Solo," she whispered.

"Try what?" he asked.

"Let's see how the relationship thing goes," she said. "No mating for life and no promises. Just us, seeing what it's like to be together."

"I'd like that," he told her, tears prickling his eyes.

"Mmm," was her only response.

Her breathing went soft and slow and he knew she had gone to sleep.

But Solo stayed awake for a long time, joy bubbling in his chest at the possibilities tomorrow offered.

12

CECILY

Cecily awoke feeling rested and content.

She opened her eyes to find herself in the motel cottage. The soft pink light of dawn filtered through the curtains.

Solo was heading into the bathroom, his towel over his shoulder, a change of clothes in his hand.

Cecily held her breath, hoping he wouldn't notice she was awake as she checked out his bare assets.

Holy crap.

He really was an amazing specimen of a man.

Her thoughts went back to last night, and the feel of his hands and mouth all over her body.

Solo closed the bathroom door quietly behind him as Cecily rolled over and buried her face in her pillow to hide her enormous smile.

This was happening. And she wasn't scared. She was actually pretty jazzed.

She hopped up and retrieved her pajamas, grinning to herself as she thought of how he'd slipped her clothes off of her like a magician.

For a guy who had never slept with a woman before, Solo had some slick moves. She wondered just how much pornography they had shown him back at the lab.

Thinking about the lab made her think about *clicking*. She wondered if it was true that sex with her would automatically make him *click* permanently into his human form and bond them together forever.

While she was nowhere near ready to think about that kind of commitment, she felt pretty crummy about leaving him high and dry last night.

She wondered if there might be a way to give him satisfaction without risking it.

The door to the bathroom swung open unexpectedly snapping her out of her pleasant thoughts. She hadn't even heard the water turn off.

Solo came out, resplendent in a white t-shirt and a pair of jeans.

"Good morning," she said.

He stared at her from across the room, his eyes smoldering just like last night.

Cecily felt her body respond instantly.

If they weren't careful, they could get stuck in this loop endlessly.

A knock at the door broke the spell.

"You guys up?" Kate's voice came through the door. "We're going to try and hit the road early."

"Yes, we're up," Cecily called back. "Give us ten minutes."

"Ten minutes and counting," Kate called back.

"I have to get dressed," Cecily said.

"You have to get dressed," Solo agreed sadly.

He stepped out of the way for her to use the bathroom.

She powered through the world's quickest shower, pulled on her clothes and dashed out.

"We still have one minute," Solo said, giving her a half-smile that made her toes curl.

She went to him, going up on her toes and twining her arms around his neck.

He wrapped his arms around her and kissed her like he was going to war.

There was another knock on the door.

"Kate sent me," Kirk called to them.

"Here we come," Cecily said.

Solo let her go and opened the door as Cecily scooped the last of her belongings into her bag.

"Good morning, brother," Kirk said politely. "Did you sleep well?"

Cecily turned around just in time to see Kirk's expression when he noticed there was only one bed.

"I slept very well," Cecily said, sweeping past the two men and out into the parking area, allowing Solo a minute to catch up with his brother.

Just ahead of her, Buck was carrying his things and Bea's in one arm, and supporting his mate around the waist with the other.

Bea wasn't a morning person. She leaned against Buck, her usually beautiful face pinched against the soft light of dawn.

"Good morning, Cecily," Buck said, grinning.

"Good morning," she replied.

They arrived at the RV at the same time. Kate was stacking water bottles into the cooler.

"Hey sleepyhead," she called to Bea.

"Mmrmmph," Bea replied, climbing into one of the double seats in the back.

Buck climbed in after her.

"You and Solo are on first shift," Kate said, handing

Cecily the keys.

"Great," Cecily said. "Did you guys eat already?"

"Already on top of that," Kate said, reaching into her backpack and fishing out a box of granola bars. "We'll eat these on the road and then stop for a good lunch. Sound good?"

"Perfect," Cecily said.

She was kind of dying to tell Kate what was going on with Solo, but he and Kirk were already approaching.

"Here are your rations," Kate said, handing over two granola bars and climbing into the RV.

Kirk climbed in after her.

Cecily turned to Solo and held out her hand with the granola bars in it.

"Your breakfast," she said.

He grabbed the keys from her other hand instead.

"You eat, I'll drive," he said.

"You don't know how to drive," she said, wondering if he was joking.

"You're kidding right?" He raised an eyebrow.

"Of course I'm not kidding," she said. "Driving is hard. I'll teach you sometime. But not today."

"I've designed, built and flown spacecraft that could travel light-years across the universe while sustaining human life. You really think I can't operate a combustion engine with a wheel?"

"I hadn't thought of it that way," Kate admitted. "But there are rules to driving."

"This thing?" He held out a dog-eared driver's manual. "I memorized it."

"Time to go, guys," Kate yelled from the back.

"Don't you want to eat your breakfast?" Solo asked.

Cecily's stomach grumbled right on cue.

"Fine," she said. "But only for half an hour. When we get closer to the city I'm taking over."

"Sure," he said, climbing into the driver's seat.

SOLO

S olo glanced over at Cecily.

She was asleep, her feet tucked up under her on the passenger seat.

Ahead of them the road spread out like a ribbon between an endless corridor of trees.

A quick peek in the rear view mirror told him that the others weren't noticing the detour he was taking.

Bea slept with her head in Buck's lap as he paged through a graphic novel.

Kate and Kirk were playing an intense game of chess at the little table.

Solo had awoken before Cecily and stolen a look at her cell phone. As he had hoped, her mom's contact was still in her address book.

From there it was only a matter of adjusting the GPS directions once she fell asleep in the RV.

Now they were headed to Greenfield, population 11,239, instead of Chicago.

Though he was sure Cecily would be surprised at first,

he hoped she would wind up feeling pleased at the sight of the place where she had grown up. Maybe she still had friends or family there, even though her mother was gone. Her mother had mentioned an uncle in the vision, and he knew he'd heard Cecily talk about an aunt.

With any luck, they would find her father, too.

The thought of reuniting Cecily with the one missing puzzle piece in her life made him feel warm and fuzzy all over.

He tried to picture what her father might look like, but he kept envisioning the man from the lemonade commercials he'd seen when studying human films on Aerie.

Instead, he focused his mind on the road ahead.

As the sun rose higher in the sky, the woods gave way to fields, and the fields to farmland. Cecily slept on beside him.

"Where are we going, brother?" Kirk asked quietly from the back.

Solo stole another glance in the rear view mirror.

Kate was listening to headphones and Buck had curled up around Bea and was napping with her.

"I thought we'd make a detour to Cecily's hometown," Solo replied.

"You're looking for her father," Kirk mused.

Solo nodded.

"So she wants to find him. That's a good thing," Kirk said.

"No," Solo said. "She doesn't know."

Kirk blew air out between his lips.

"You think it's a bad idea?" Solo asked.

"I guess we'll find out when she wakes up," Kirk said.

Solo watched a sign approach.

GREENFIELD **2** MILES

AS IF ON CUE, Cecily began to stir in the seat beside him.

Solo fixed his eyes on the road, resolved. If she got mad at him that was okay. He was going to fill the hole in her heart. And then there would be a place for him in it.

C ecily awoke when the rumble of the RV stopped. She squinted against the light.

Something was off.

She looked around.

Everyone in the RV was looking back at her.

"Hey guys," she said, mystified.

"Hello," Solo said, smiling at her. "I have a surprise for you."

"Um, okay." Cecily tried to imagine what that could be.

After last night, the only surprises she could think of were definitely not the kind to be shared in front of her friends.

The view out the window hit her.

She was home.

Not the studio in Queens - her old home, Greenfield.

"Why are we here?" she asked, blinking the sleep out of her eyes.

"I wanted to see the place where you grew up," Solo said. "I thought you might like to visit as well."

"I told you I didn't want to come back here," Cecily said.

She began to get a panicky feeling. Tears prickled her eyes.

"We were passing right by anyway, and we left so early. I thought we could afford a detour for a few hours," Solo said.

"Let's stretch our legs," Kate said softly to the others in the back.

Cecily bit her lip and gazed out the window as her friends exited the RV.

Solo had pulled the RV in beside one of the town parks. Cecily remembered rollerblading around it when she was a kid, with the family dog on a leash. She had come home with so many skinned knees. Birds sang in the maples that lined the perimeter of the park, just as they always had.

"You waited until I was asleep and then you did something I asked you not to do," she said as calmly as she could.

"I thought that you might really want to do this," Solo said. "I thought that you might want to explore your past."

"There's nothing to explore in my past," Cecily said bitterly. "It's all gone."

She turned away from him to gather her thoughts. She would go retrieve the others and they could get back on the road and try to put this all behind them, in every sense.

"Cecily, there's something I need to tell you," Solo said earnestly.

His calm voice was even deeper than usual.

She turned back to him, curious in spite of her anger.

"My brothers and I have certain... gifts," he said carefully.

"Sure you do," Cecily said, rolling her eyes. "Look, you're good in bed, but that doesn't mean you can play games with me."

"Oh," he laughed nervously. "That's not what I meant. But thank you."

"Go on," she said.

"These gifts are more like... well, I guess you would call them powers," he said. "Things no human can do. We think that they may have manifested as a vestige of our personal strengths on Aerie."

"Super powers?" Cecily asked incredulously.

"Well, some are more super than others," Solo said. "But yes, enhanced abilities."

"So what's yours?" Cecily asked.

"It's hard to explain," he said. "But I guess I would describe it as reading object memories."

"What are object memories?" Cecily asked her anger almost forgotten in the face of this new discovery.

"Well, for example, I grabbed your backpack the other day instead of Kirk's and I touched the keychain," Solo said. "And I saw... I saw your mother give you the bracelet."

Cecily stared at him. He appeared to be telling the truth.

"Wait, no, *I* told you about the bracelet," she said.

"You were crying in your bed the night before Father's Day breakfast," Solo said softly, looking down at his hands. "And your mother told you that your uncle would come to the breakfast with you. And you asked her about your father and she wouldn't answer. Instead she gave you the bracelet."

Cecily froze.

He had described the scene exactly, with details she certainly hadn't shared with him, or anyone for that matter.

"Dr. Bhimani said we should not tell anyone about our gifts until we were mated," Solo said sadly. "But I don't feel I have a choice. You have a right to know."

"Thank you," Cecily said automatically. She was still processing what he had said.

"And I'm sorry that touching your things can be an invasion of your privacy," Solo continued.

"That's why you didn't want to hold my stuff," she said, putting it together.

"Most times I can control my gift," Solo told her "But when it comes to the people I care about, sometimes the object memories just happen, whether I want them to or not."

She nodded, trying to imagine what it would be like to see memories by touching things.

"At any rate, I saw that you want to know more about your father," Solo said. "And with my gift, I thought if we came here, maybe I could help you find what you want."

Cecily looked out at the park again.

A little girl and her brother were trying to fly a kite, leaves dancing on the tree branches above them as their dad looked on from one of the benches.

She had longed to see her own dad on that bench once upon a time. Would she still want to see him now?

The feelings bubbled up in her chest again, as strong as they had ever been. Anger, loss, and a burning curiosity. The only way to stop the volcano of emotion was to not think about it.

"If you knew about him, maybe you would feel better," Solo said softly.

She wondered if that could be true.

"Okay," she sighed. "Okay."

"Okay, what?" Solo asked.

"Okay, let's do this," she said. "Let's look for him. Let's try to figure this out."

"Really?" Solo asked, his eyes dancing.

"Really," she replied. "But we've only got a day, so let's not get too optimistic."

"We'd better get started," he pointed out.

"Not yet," Cecily said. "There's something you have to understand."

"Okay," Solo said. "What is it?"

"You can never do this again," she said.

"Never use my gift?" he asked.

"No," she said. "Your gift can be invasive, but it's part of who you are. I'm talking about the fact that I told you I didn't want to come here and you tricked me. That's not okay. From here on in, you need to be honest with me, and know that when I say no I mean no. Do you understand?"

"I understand, Cecily" he said, nodding solemnly. I will not try to trick you again."

"If you do, it's over," she told him, giving him a stern look to make sure he knew she wasn't kidding.

He nodded again, reproachfully. He looked so much like a sad puppy that she had to resist cracking a smile and undermining her own message.

"Okay," she said, hopping out of the RV.

The other four were huddled together on the sidewalk opposite the park. They looked up at her as one, like a herd of startled deer.

"It's okay," she said. "Get back in and we'll explain on the way to my storage unit."

15

CECILY

Cecily finished re-taping the last box and straightened up, brushing off her hands.

"It's a bust," she said.

"Now what?" Kate asked from the hallway outside the tiny storage locker. She and Kirk had just rejoined them after securing them all rooms at the only thing resembling a hotel in town, the Greenville Inn.

"I'm not sure," Cecily said. "If nothing in here brought on a memory of my dad, I don't know where I'd have to go to find one. I don't have any more of my mom's stuff anywhere."

Solo's expression was unreadable.

She wondered if maybe he had seen something after all.

"What about your house?" Bea asked.

"I sold it," Cecily said. "There's another family living there now."

"Do you know them?" Kate asked. "Would they let us visit? Just in case there is some kind of clue there."

"No, and no," Cecily said. "I was still kind of hurting

about my mom when I sold the house. I never met the people. The estate attorney signed everything for me. But I wasn't the most pleasant negotiator. I don't think they would have much reason to help me."

"But they never actually saw you?" Bea asked.

Cecily shook her head.

"So we pretend to be from the gas company," Bea said.

"Oh, like *101 Dalmatians*," Buck put in excitedly.

"Uh, yeah," Bea said, less excitedly. "Kind of like that."

"But we won't take any puppies, right?" Buck asked.

"Of course not," Bea assured him.

"It's a good plan then." He nodded sagely.

"We need costumes," Kate said.

"I've got a couple of coveralls I use when I'm building props," Cecily said.

"This seems risky," Kate said.

"The worst thing that can happen is that they try to call the gas company and we make a break for it," Bea said.

"What do you think, Solo?" Cecily asked. "If we can get you in there can you get a reading off something like a wall or a door?"

"I saw you after touching the kitchen counter back in Philadelphia," Solo replied. "It was before I even met you, Cecily."

She felt the blood rush to her cheeks.

"Okay, let's do this," Kate announced, buying Cecily a moment to recover.

Cecily secured the storage locker and they all headed out to the RV.

Half an hour later, they were pulling up in front of the brick Cape Cod where Cecily had grown up.

She noticed that the flowering azaleas were still in the

beds in the front of the house. The new owners had put up a porch swing and planted a row of baby evergreens that would one day block the neighbors' driveway.

Her mom had always talked about doing that.

"You okay?" Kate asked.

Cecily nodded as they approached the door.

"I'll handle this," Bea said, marching forward.

Cecily fought the urge to giggle.

Bea always wore black satin, leather or lace. Her goth style was epic. But in preparation for her role as a gas company representative, Bea had borrowed a hot pink polo shirt and a pair of khakis from Kate. She actually looked pretty professional, but to anyone who knew the real Beatrix Li, the difference was comical.

Bea knocked on the door.

A moment later a woman opened it. She had short blonde hair and a baby on her hip.

"Can I help you?" she asked.

"We're here from the gas company, ma'am," Beatrix said. "One of your neighbors called in a leak. Have you smelled gas anywhere in your residence?"

"No," the woman replied, her eyes wide.

"This is number 816, right?" Beatrix asked, consulting her clipboard. "Sandra and Robert Winthrop?"

"That's us," the woman said. "Wow."

"Don't be alarmed, ma'am," Bea said. "Sometimes a pedestrian just gets a whiff of something when they're walking. It doesn't always mean a gas leak, or if there is one, it doesn't necessarily mean it's in your home. But we can't be too safe."

"Of course not," Sandra said. "Do you need to come in?"

"What's going on?" a man's voice asked from inside.

"Gas leak, Bob, they have to check the house," Sandra called back.

"Wow," Bob said. "You want to take the baby outside, Sandy?"

The woman stepped inside and opened the door for Beatrix, who gestured the others in.

Kirk and Solo stepped inside and Cecily followed. Kate and Buck were in the RV around the corner, prepared to be the getaway drivers if the need arose. She didn't think it would come to that, but she also didn't want to risk someone recognizing Kate from her TV show.

"Wouldn't we smell gas?" Sandy worried.

"You might think so," Beatrix said. "But it takes only the tiniest pinhole leak to present a risk. So we don't rely on our noses. We use gas leak detection meters."

Buck waved around his detection meter for them to see.

It was really just a prop Cecily had thrown together from her own supplies and the contents of the toolbox on the RV. Solo had one too. They wouldn't hold up to close inspection, so Cecily told the guys to keep them moving around as much as possible.

As Beatrix drew out the Winthrop family in a conversation about natural gas safety, Solo headed for the stairs.

He waved his detector around with one hand while patting the walls and woodwork with his other.

He looked a bit like he was pretending to be blind. Cecily hoped he was getting readings.

"I'm going to check upstairs," he said.

She followed him up.

"Which room was your mother's?" he whispered.

She pointed him down the hall to the room overlooking the front yard.

He touched the knob and the doorframe.

He went over to the window and placed his hands on the frame.

Cecily watched as Solo's eyes closed and a shiver went over his big body.

He was seeing something, she was sure of it.

There were sounds on the stairs. She hoped it was only Bea and Kirk. But of course it was the owner.

"What's he doing?" Bob asked from the doorway.

"Oh, um, he has a good nose for this," Cecily said. "He didn't get a reading, but he's got a hunch. Give him a sec."

"Wow, good talent for the job, huh?" Bob asked.

"I'm going outside with the baby, hon," Sandy called from downstairs.

"Okay," Bob said.

He stood, gazing at Solo in fascination.

They weren't going to get the house to themselves.

Suddenly Solo straightened.

"Did you pick up a gas scent?" Cecily asked quickly.

Solo blinked and turned to face his audience.

"Nope," he said. "And the meter's not getting anything either. You're safe."

"Aren't you going to check the basement?" Bob sounded mystified.

But Solo had already walked past him and was heading down the stairs.

"No, we got the readings we needed," Bea said.

They crossed through the living room and out into the yard, where Sandy stood by the azaleas with the baby.

Cecily thought of the pictures her mom had taken of her in front of the flowers each year and got a lump in her throat.

"That was quick," Sandy said.

"Thank you very much for your cooperation," Bea said. "There's no need to worry. This was a false alarm situation."

"Geez, what a day," Sandy said. "First the guy from the movies, and now a false alarm gas leak. What's next?"

"Oh, I'm not so sure that was him, hon," Bob said. "Just because he had sunglasses on doesn't mean he was from Hollywood."

"What guy from the movies?" Bea asked.

Sandy looked thoughtful for a moment.

"Shoot, I can't remember his name," she said.

"It wasn't him," Bob said. "Anyway, I'm sure you guys have more important things to do."

They headed back into the house, still arguing pleasantly over whether they had seen a movie star or just a man with sunglasses.

"I guess there's not much to do in this town, huh?" Bea teased Cecily.

"Do you think they really saw a movie star?" Buck asked.

"There hasn't been a movie star in this town in years," Cecily said. "At least not until Kate got here this morning."

Solo was quiet.

"Did you get anything useful?" she asked him.

"Maybe," he said. "It was very faint. I saw her outside somewhere, with a man, but his back was turned."

"Why would touching her window give you a memory of somewhere else?" Cecily asked.

"It's not an exact science," Solo told her. "Maybe she spent time looking out the window and thinking about the place I saw. It is possible that if we go to wherever they were, I could get a stronger reading. But I don't know where it is."

"What did it look like?" Cecily asked, grasping at straws. She was surprised at how disappointed she felt.

"It was a wide open space, with huge rocks," he said.

"Greenfield Gorge," Cecily exclaimed.

"Do you know where it is?" he asked.

"Absolutely," she said, her excitement returning. "Let's go."

16

SOLO

S olo climbed out of the RV and looked around.

It was strange to visit a place that shared so many qualities with Aerie and yet was so different.

A wide expanse of brown rocks and crags spread out before him. Sunlight bounced off the stones, its quality so cool and far away compared with the blazing white starlight of his former home.

The ground between the rocks was clay dirt, not sand, but it had the same dry and dusty quality.

"This is where *My Red Hot Alien Summer* was filmed," Bea said reverently, looking around.

"This doesn't look like it," Buck said dubiously.

"They used gels in the lighting to change the color," Bea explained. "Try to picture it as more red."

"Oh," Buck said. "I see."

Cecily climbed up on a large rock and surveyed the valley below. She stood with her feet wide and her shoulders thrown back. The breeze tumbled her curls over her shoulder and Solo thought she looked like the drawings of Greek goddesses in Dr. Bhimani's library back in Stargazer.

"Have you found anything, brother?" Kirk called to him.

Solo remembered himself, shook his head and wandered through the crags, trying to find the outcropping where he had seen Cecily's mother.

It had been vague, a memory of a memory. He wondered if she had really stood by the window, stroking the frame and thinking of her lost love, or if he had gotten it all wrong.

Solo didn't want to disappoint Cecily, but he had never tried to pick up a particular memory before.

For the most part, he tried not to pick up memories at all. He had been given to understand that the invasion of privacy was impolite. On Aerie a single instance of bad manners might be social suicide.

Here on Earth he knew the rules were looser, but it was hard to relax his own manners even if others would accept it. Besides, he had no wish to intrude on anyone's private thoughts. The things he had seen were often confusing and sometimes frightening.

But if his power could help Cecily, then he might actually begin to think of it as a gift instead of a curse.

He reached the edge of the precipice and turned back.

That was when he saw it.

Somehow, Cecily had chosen to stand on the exact rock her mother had been leaning against in the memory. He had been looking at it from the wrong angle.

He approached her, shading his eyes from the sun.

"Hey," she said.

"Hey," he replied. "I was looking for the rock your mom was leaning against. But you were standing on it the whole time."

"Should I get down?" she asked.

"No, I'm just going to touch it," he told her.

Solo closed his eyes and pictured Cecily's mother. He

reached out with his hand and his mind at the same time.

The moment his hand touched the rock the scene around him went dim.

Stars glimmered in the sky above.

Cecily's mother, Agnes Page, reclined against the rock in front of him.

A man stood before her.

"I really like you," he said in a voice that was somehow familiar to Solo. "But the acting lifestyle is difficult. I travel all the time. I'll be gone tomorrow and who knows where after that?"

"I don't care," Agnes said, reaching her hand up to cup his cheek.

"You're a nice girl, I don't want to hurt you," the man said softly.

Solo backed up, hoping the vision would hold.

As he moved, the man groaned in surrender.

Solo slid to the side to try and get a better look at him. But the man's face was now blocked by Cecily's mom's hair as they kissed.

Though the vision was a shadowy ghost compared to real life, Solo could see that the man was tall and lean.

At last they pulled back from the kiss.

Solo nearly gasped.

Though the man was decades older now, Solo would have recognized that face anywhere.

And in this context, it suddenly struck him how odd it was that none of them had figured it out before.

Cecily had obviously gotten her curls and her smile from her mom.

But she had the exact same constellation of freckles across the bridge of her nose as her father.

Dirk Malcolm.

17

SOLO

S olo let go of the rock. Let go of the past.

The sunlight of the present day crashed into his face.

"Are you okay?" Cecily asked, scrambling down to join him.

The others gathered around.

He looked into the eyes of the woman he loved more than anything in the world, wondering where he would find the strength to tell her the truth.

He closed his eyes and pictured the man again.

It was definitely Dirk.

In a way, it made sense. He had filmed a movie right where they were standing. He would have had ample time to interact with residents of the town.

But he remembered Cecily saying that her aunt was the one to have an affair with the movie star.

Could Dirk Malcolm have had affairs with *both* sisters?

It occurred to Solo that maybe the vision he had just seen was a vision of Cecily's aunt and not her mother at all. Maybe he had picked up one of her memories at the house.

He'd seen pictures of Cecily's mom, but not her aunt. He wondered if the two women looked alike. Cecily shared her mother's curls. Maybe they ran in the family and everything he had just seen meant nothing.

"What is it?" Cecily asked. "What did you see?"

"I'm - I'm not sure," he hedged. "Do you still have family in this town?"

"Yeah," Cecily said. "My Uncle Ray moved to Portland when I was in high school, but my Aunt Stacy's here. She still has the nail salon on Main Street."

"Can we go see her?" Solo asked.

"Sure," Cecily said. "Absolutely. Come on, guys."

He could see the worry in her eyes. But until he learned more, there was nothing Solo could do to ease it.

Cecily drove, a look of resolve on her face.

Solo was glad she was determined, glad she wanted to know the truth. If it could be found today, he would find it for her.

At last they pulled up in a small downtown area.

Cecily parked the RV and they all piled out.

The town library had handsome marble columns, otherwise it was a modest town square filled with glass storefronts and metal benches.

Cecily set off in the direction of a shop with the words *Greenfield Nail Salon* on the awning above it.

"We'll go to the cafe down the block," Kate told Solo. "You go on with her. Let us know if you need us."

Solo nodded and entered the nail salon after Cecily.

Solo noticed the scent of chemicals, then the line of women sitting on large chairs with their feet in small pools of water.

"Cecily?"

A woman stepped from behind the cash register. She

was very tall, with stick-straight brown hair and big brown eyes.

"Aunt Stacy," Cecily said warmly.

The two women embraced and Solo felt their happiness in his heart. At the same time, he knew that this was not the woman from his vision.

"What are you doing here, honey?" Aunt Stacy asked.

"We need to talk privately," Cecily said.

"Come on back," her aunt said.

"Come on, Solo," Cecily said.

They all followed behind the curtain to a surprisingly bright room with glass doors overlooking a small grassy courtyard. There was a table at the center of the room with two half full water glasses on it. The counter top next to the table held a coffee maker and a row of mugs.

"Do you guys want something to drink?" Aunt Stacy asked.

"We're fine," Cecily said. "This is my friend, Solo. We came here because... because he needs to ask you a few questions."

"Oh, okay," Aunt Stacy said, giving Solo an appreciative once-over. "Nice to meet you. I hope you kids are staying in town for a while. You're welcome to my guest room."

"It is a pleasure to meet you as well," Solo told her honestly. He would have preferred they meet under less auspicious circumstances, but he was glad to have the chance to connect with someone important to Cecily.

"Well, what would you like to ask me?"

He considered. There did not seem to be a mannerly way to ask her what he needed to know.

"Cecily tells me that you once... *dated* Dirk Malcolm when he was filming a movie in this town," he said at last. "Is that true?"

"Oh," she said, looking less surprised than he would have expected. "Um, yes, Dirk was here to film a movie and that rumor certainly spread around this town like wildfire."

That was an answer and also *not* an answer.

"Was the rumor true?" Solo asked.

Aunt Stacy bit her lip.

Solo looked down at the table to give her a moment to compose herself. He hoped that she would want her niece to have the truth.

The sunlight from outside hit the water glass in front of him, shooting a glare into his eye.

He reached out and pushed it away.

A clear image of Dirk Malcolm holding the cup dropped down around him.

"He was here," Solo said, letting go of the glass.

"Here? But, you didn't even have this place back then," Cecily said.

"No, he was here today," Solo said. "Earlier this afternoon."

"Oh, Cecily," Aunt Stacy said, "I...I..."

She began to cry into her hands.

Solo grabbed the water glass and closed his eyes to let the curtain of memory fall around him.

Dirk Malcolm stood in the doorway of the room.

Stacy poured two glasses of water into the cups, glancing up at him nervously.

"Stacy, I wouldn't have recognized you," Dirk said.

"Oh boy," Aunt Stacy said. "You'd better sit down."

"I never stopped thinking about you," Dirk told her.

"Well, you're wrong about that," Stacy told him. "I need to explain something."

"Listen, there's nothing to explain," Dirk said. "I was

young and dumb. I didn't know my butt from a hole in the ground—"

"—I'm not her," Stacy yelled.

"You... I'm sorry, what?" Dirk asked.

"My name is Stacy Page, but you didn't sleep with me, you slept with my sister," Aunt Stacy said.

"I—I did?" he asked.

"Her name was Agnes, after our grandmother," Stacy said, handing him the glass of water and indicating the seat in front of him. "But she always hated that name. Thought it made her sound like an old lady."

"Agnes," Dirk echoed.

"When you approached her, she freaked out and gave you my name instead. She never thought hers was cool, and she wanted to impress you, I guess."

Aunt Stacy smiled fondly.

"Wow," Dirk said. "Where is she now? Is she still in town?"

"No," Aunt Stacy shook her head.

"Doesn't matter," Dirk said. "Wherever she is, I'll go there and find her. I was young and stupid when we met. *My Red Hot Alien Summer* was the first movie I ever headlined. I thought all I cared about was my career, and that a good woman like your sister wouldn't be able to keep up with my lifestyle. I know better now. I would trade it all for another chance to be with her. I've always felt like I left a piece of myself here with her. I'm sure she's settled down with someone else, but I still want to tell her how much she meant to me."

"Oh, Dirk," Aunt Stacy said, tears brimming in her eyes. "She passed away four years ago."

There was a moment of silence and then Dirk Malcolm dropped his head into his hands and his shoulders racked with big, ugly sobs. This was real and horrible - nothing like the movie, where a single tear ran down his manly squared jaw.

Solo couldn't help but feel he was intruding on a moment not meant for his eyes. He removed his hand from the glass and looked to Cecily's aunt.

"Her mother begged me not to tell," she said helplessly. "Everyone already said I was a wild child anyway. And she was always such a good girl."

"Do you want to tell her or should I?" he asked.

"Her mother didn't want her to know," Stacy pleaded.

"I want her to know," he said.

18

CECILY

Cecily looked back and forth between her aunt and the man she was learning to love. Something terrible was passing between them and the truth of it was shimmering just out of her reach.

Solo turned to her.

"Do you want the truth?" he asked.

"Yes," she told him without hesitation.

"Your father is Dirk Malcolm," he said.

Cecily blinked.

"No, he had a fling with Aunt Stacy," she said.

"No," Aunt Stacy said. "He had a fling with your mother."

"I don't understand," Cecily said.

"Your mom and I were still living at home with Grandma and Grandpa," Aunt Stacy said. "Your mom was a senior in high school, I was nineteen and working at the hair salon. When they came here to film that movie the whole town went crazy. "

"You guys used to talk about that," Cecily said.

"Anyway, your mom met Dirk at the record store," Aunt

Stacy went on. "She was young and so lovely and shy. But they took to each other immediately. When he asked her name she got nervous and gave him mine instead."

"She never liked being Agnes," Cecily said.

"Exactly," Aunt Stacy said. "They snuck off together whenever they could. On his last night in town, I slept in her bed so she could go out with him."

"You had a later curfew because you were older," Cecily guessed.

"Yeah," Aunt Stacy said. "Or because I was a lost cause." She laughed and rolled her eyes. "Anyway, they had quite a romantic evening out at the gorge. But he told her before anything happened that his career was taking off and that he wasn't in a good place to have a relationship. She knew what she was getting into. She made her choices in spite of that."

Cecily nodded. That sounded like her mom, fair and practical, but not a person to cut the fun out of her life.

"She took him at his word," Aunt Stacy said. "And though she shed some tears when they all left town, she never held it against him. He'd been honest with her. She would only say that she missed him and wished she had something to remember him by."

Cecily bit her lip.

"She missed her period the next month," Aunt Stacy said. "I went to the drug store for her and got her a test. Sure enough, she was pregnant. So he had left her something to remember him by after all."

Solo put a hand on Cecily's back and she was grateful for the comfort.

"Dirk sent her a whole bunch of letters in the months after that," Aunt Stacy said. "But your mother would never have allowed him to give up his career for you two. She knew he was too honorable not to do the right thing by her if he ever found out about you. So she ignored the letters and soon enough they stopped coming. I know because they were all addressed to me. She never did tell him the truth about her name. Of course Coleen at the post office couldn't keep her mouth shut, so the whole town new about it before long. It was good thing he had my name, or it would have all been too obvious. Even as it was, I was pretty surprised no one ever put it together."

"Wow," Cecily breathed.

"And your mom did give you a good life, all by herself, didn't she?" Aunt Stacy asked.

"She sure did," Cecily nodded.

"Anyway, I have no idea how, but your boyfriend is right. Dirk did come here today. He left not an hour ago," Aunt Stacy went on. "He wasn't looking for you, and I didn't tell him anything about a child. But he did let me know that I could reach out to him if I ever needed anything, and if I ever wanted to talk about your mom."

Aunt Stacy pulled a card out of her pocket and slid it across the table. "In case you want to call him yourself."

Cecily shook her head, and stood up.

"Please don't be angry with him, Cecily," Aunt Stacy said. "He doesn't know. He loved her. He just didn't realize it in time. And... and please don't be too angry with me either. My little sister was my world. I couldn't break her trust. I love you, Cecily."

Cecily bit back her anger and her sadness.

"I'm upset, Aunt Stacy," she said carefully. "But I'll get over it. Right now I need to leave."

"I understand, honey," Aunt Stacy said. "I'll be here when you're ready. Whenever that is."

Cecily nodded and headed through the curtains and into the nail salon, and from there out onto the sidewalk.

She could hear Solo jogging to catch up with her.

"Do you want to tell everyone what's going on, or should I?" Solo asked gently.

She turned and saw that their friends were approaching, looking curious.

"I don't know if I'm ready to talk about it," she said. "Would you mind filling them in? I just kind of want to sit down for a minute."

"Of course," he said, squeezing her shoulders and pressing his lips to the top of her head.

Cecily lowered herself onto the bench overlooking Main Street as Solo headed toward their friends.

She took a deep breath, then let it sink in.

Dirk Malcolm is my father.

Cecily had wanted to know who her father was ever since she could remember, and the truth was that he was someone she had met professionally once or twice. She knew what he looked like. She knew the sound of his voice.

Hell, he was going to be in the movie she and her friends were working on. How was she going to deal with that?

All the information she'd spent a lifetime craving was hers now.

She looked out over the village streets she'd walked as a child, always thinking the sunshine would seem brighter, and the birds would sing more sweetly if she only knew who her father was.

And now she did.

But it was funny. The world seemed just the same as before.

19

SOLO

Solo approached Cecily.

She was still sitting on the bench, gazing out over the street, just as she'd been when he'd left her to tell their friends the news.

They had all gone back to the cafe to grab an early dinner and give her a bit of space.

Cecily looked calmer than he had expected, given her recent news. But she didn't necessarily look happy.

Solo was generally very pleased with the ability of the human facial muscles to indicate every possible gradation of emotion. But this was something else, this calm, blank look. He wondered if she might be meditating to prevent herself from becoming over-excited.

"They're all very happy for you," he told her softly as he sat down beside her. "And you must be excited too."

Cecily didn't respond.

"I can't believe that he is right here in this town," Solo went on. "Or certainly close by if he was at your aunt's place just an hour ago. If we call him now maybe you can meet here, in the place where he knew your mother."

"No," Cecily said.

Solo was so taken aback he didn't know what to say. He waited, hoping she would help him understand.

But she remained as still as a star.

"Why not?" he asked her at last. "I thought you wanted to know your father."

"Dirk Malcolm epitomizes everything that makes me not want a man in my life in the first place," Cecily said. "He's the ultimate non-committal playboy."

Solo gazed at his love.

He hadn't recognized happiness in her face because what was there was resignation.

"It sounds like maybe Dirk has changed his mind about what he wants in his life," Solo said.

"I don't want to be his guinea pig," Cecily said. "I found the answer I thought I wanted. Now I just want to get out of town as soon as possible."

"Don't you want to give him a chance?" Solo asked. "Give yourself a chance to see what having him in your life would be like?"

"I don't," Cecily said.

"Are you sure?" Solo asked.

"I don't want to talk about it anymore," Cecily said.

Her eyes were as dull as her expression. He had never seen her this way. As long as he'd known her, that mischievous spark had danced in her eyes. Now it had vanished.

"Okay," he said. "Go ahead and join the others. Grab something to eat. I'll take the RV to the gas station and pick you guys up afterward."

"Thank you for understanding," Cecily said softly.

Solo nodded, though he didn't understand at all.

He watched her as she walked back toward the cafe, afternoon sun setting her auburn curls alight.

His hand was in the pocket of his jeans, worrying the edge of a bit of paper.

Her words from this morning echoed in his head.

If you try to trick me again it's over.

He pulled the card out of his pocket and looked at it. He had grabbed it from Aunt Stacy's table, then jogged after Cecily. She didn't know he had it.

The front of the card had Dirk's photograph. He was smiling. The constellation of freckles across the bridge of his nose was the same as Cecily's.

Solo flipped the card over.

On the back a phone number was neatly jotted. Dirk's personal line.

Solo ran a hand through his hair.

He had a choice to make.

If he called Dirk and told him everything, he would lose Cecily forever. She had told him herself that if he tricked her again it was over.

If he let her crush down her feelings and move on without talking to Dirk, maybe she would eventually come around and be Solo's mate. But she would never really have the answers she needed. Never really be able to move on with him.

Solo sighed.

If the choice was to lose her or to live with a half-version of her, there was no choice at all.

It wasn't about him.

It was about helping Cecily.

20

CECILY

Cecily jogged through the town square toward the park.

Dark storm clouds were forming overhead and the scent of rain filled the air.

She had been halfway through her meal when Kirk whispered to her that Solo needed her to meet him as quickly as possible at the little park where they'd stopped on the way in. He'd told her to meet Solo under the weeping willow.

Cecily tried to imagine what Solo could possibly want. As far as she could figure it he either wanted to break up, to mate, or to try and convince her one last time to confront her father.

None of those options appealed to her.

For all that men accused women of being drama queens, in Cecily's experience, women were pretty laid back. It was men who were always declaring their intentions, demanding answers and summoning a person to a strange meeting place when all she wanted was to eat her soup and sandwich in peace.

She reached the park and headed over to the willow. As a child she had loved hiding under its branches.

She entered that shaded space but Solo wasn't there.

A piece of paper rustled against the trunk of the tree.

Cecily grabbed it.

DEAR CECILY,

If I hadn't seen the vision of you as a child I wouldn't have understood how much you needed to know more about your father. I did not mean to take that memory from you, but I did. And I can't unsee what I saw.

You deserve to know your father.

And, Cecily, I think he deserves to know you too.

I haven't told him who you are to him. But by the time you read this, he will be waiting at the park bench.

Whether or not you go to him will be your choice.

Yes, I have deceived you again and I know what that means. I am going back to Stargazer to turn myself in to the lab. You won't have to see me again.

If this meeting brings you peace, it will have been worth it.

I will always love you, Cecily.

YOURS,

Solo

CECILY TUCKED the letter into her pocket.

He was out there. For better or worse, her father was out there.

She took a deep breath and stepped out of the protective shade of the willow.

"Agnes?" someone called out brokenly.

She turned, surprised to hear her mother's name, and saw Dirk Malcolm sitting on the bench, right where Solo had said he would be. The sunlight brought out the rusty highlights in his hair.

"Sorry, you look like someone I know," he said.

She studied him a moment, trying to decide.

"Wait." His eyes lit up. "I *do* know you. Cecily Page, right? Beatrix Li's friend, the special-effects guru. What are you doing here?"

It was easier than she'd expected to go to him.

"This is my home town," she explained.

"Wow," he said. "That's crazy."

"What are you doing here?" she asked.

"I was trying to right an old wrong," he told her.

"Maybe I can help," she said. "Let's sit down."

He sat on the bench and patted the seat beside him.

Cecily's heart lurched as she thought about the many times she would have loved to have had him there to do that, back when she was small. She marveled at how many little wounds a parent's love could heal.

"My mother lived here," she told him. "And so did I, until after I graduated."

"Wait," Dirk said. "Wait... Are you... Agnes's daughter?"

Cecily nodded, noticing the constellation of freckles across his nose and wondering how long it would take him to notice hers.

"Of course you are. You look like her," he said. "I thought you were her just now. Isn't that funny? Of course, I knew her when she was very young. She was a wonderful woman."

"She was a wonderful mom," Cecily agreed.

"I'm so sorry for your loss," he told her.

Cecily swallowed down the lump that suddenly formed in her throat.

"What was her life like?" Dirk asked. "Was she happy?"

Cecily smiled. "Yes, she was happy. She had a good life. She worked at her sister's salon. Everyone in town loved her. I loved her."

"I loved her too," Dirk said.

"I know," Cecily said.

"Is your dad still around?" Dirk asked.

"She never got married," Cecily said carefully.

"She didn't?" Dirk asked, eyebrows raised.

"There was someone she loved once, I think, a long time ago," Cecily said. "She always said I looked just like him, though most people say I look like her."

His eyes widened and she saw the exact second when he noticed her freckles, his hand moving up to his face to trace his own.

"Are you...?" he couldn't finish the question.

"We can stand up, walk away, and pretend this never happened," Cecily offered.

But Dirk's face had gone pink and he was holding his arms out to her, his eyes bright with tears.

Cecily was surprised to find that she did want to hug him. She went into his arms, wondering at the scent of his retro aftershave. He smelled like she'd always imagined a TV dad would smell.

He pressed a tender kiss on the top of her head and she could feel hot tears falling in her hair.

Cecily found herself crying too, then sobbing into his chest.

"Thank you," he whispered through his tears. "Thank you so much for telling me. I'm so glad about this, and I hope... I hope you have a place in your life for me. I'll try not to embarrass you in front of your friends, or wreck your life or anything."

Cecily found herself laughing. She pulled away.

Dirk let her go, but kept hold of her hand as he dug in his pocket and pulled out a tissue.

"Thanks," Cecily said, taking it.

"Why didn't she tell me?" Dirk asked.

"She knew you were a good guy," Cecily sniffed. "She could see your career was taking off."

"I would have given anything, everything..." he said, shaking his head. "I would have loved for the three of us to be together."

"She was trying to protect you," Cecily told him. "That's why she didn't tell you."

"So your aunt told you I was here?" he asked.

"No," Cecily said. "Well, yes, after I confronted her... But I still wouldn't have told you. I'm only here because of Solo. He helped me figure out that you were my father. And then he tricked me into this meeting. He thought I needed to meet you. He was convinced that I would feel better if I did."

"And do you?" Dirk asked.

"Well... yeah," she said, realizing that she felt more than better. She felt excited, happy even.

"You're lucky to be in a loving relationship with someone like him," Dirk said.

"I'm not in a relationship," Cecily admitted.

"Why not?" Dirk asked.

"I told him I would break up with him if he tried to trick me into anything," Cecily said. "The note he left me here in the park says he knows I'm breaking up with him for this, and so he's leaving."

"Do you want to know what I think of this guy?" Dirk asked.

Cecily nodded.

"I think you're lucky to have someone in your life who loves you so much they are willing to sacrifice their own happiness for yours," he said.

"It wasn't going to work out anyway," Cecily said.

"Why wouldn't it?"

"You know how the show biz life is. It's nothing but traveling, a new city every week or every month," Cecily said. "And I love it. I can't picture myself doing anything else."

Her father was suddenly on his knees at her feet.

"Cecily," he said, with tears in his eyes for the second time. "Please don't make the same mistake I did. I know I don't have the right to advise you as your dad, but I'm begging you as someone who cares about you. If you love him, you can't let him go. Don't wind up like me."

"Oh my god," she said, the clouds in her mind suddenly parting to reveal the truth. "Oh my god, I have to go find him!"

"Yes, you do," Dirk sprang to his feet. "Come on, my car's across the street. Where would he be?"

21

SOLO

Solo stood at the bus stop.

Rain was beginning to fall, fat drops soaking into his hair and splashing in the puddles that were already forming in the macadam of the shopping center parking lot. Thunder rumbled in the distance.

He didn't care that he was cold and wet. He was numb at the thought of leaving Cecily. Already his heart felt stretched tight like a rubber band between where he stood and where she was now.

He tried to picture her with her father. Would she tell Dirk who she was to him?

Though she had indicated that she didn't want Dirk in her life in that way, Solo couldn't picture her pushing him away. He had heard the sadness in the man's voice when he'd called and asked him to go to the park if he wanted to right an old wrong.

He imagined Cecily smiling, her father embracing her. He imagined her happy, opening her heart to love and commitment one day. He imagined her in a wedding dress, her father giving her away to a faceless groom. He imagined her nursing a child with russet curls, happy.

These visions threatened to rip his soul to shreds, but they were all he had now. The hope of her happiness would have to be enough.

He looked up when he heard a vehicle pulling in to the parking lot, thinking it must be the bus.

But it was a silver Lexus. It seemed to be traveling far too quickly.

He watched in amazement as its brakes squealed and it slid sideways into a parking spot like something out of a movie.

The door burst open and someone flung themselves out of the passenger side, auburn curls bouncing, a hand shielding her blue eyes from the rain.

Cecily.

He ran to her, his heart pounding.

She melted into his arms.

"I'm sorry," she panted. "I'm so sorry. I love you."

A crushing weight he hadn't realized he was carrying suddenly lifted and he felt like he could fly.

"Cecily," he said helplessly, "Cecily."

She pulled away slightly and looked into his eyes.

"I accept you as my mate," she said.

The thunder stopped mid-boom and soft sunlight embraced them.

Solo blinked, not understanding.

Cecily's eyes widened.

"The glade," she whispered.

He tore his eyes from hers to look around.

The parking lot was gone. In its place was a grassy meadow, trees swaying at its perimeters. Birds chirped overhead and a soft breeze lifted Cecily's curls.

"I used to come here when I was a kid," she said. "This is what was here before the parking lot. Are you doing this?"

He shook his head. "I can't do this," he told her. "I mean, I can see a memory vision, but only a shadow, a ghost image. This must be you."

"What do you mean?" she asked.

"When you accepted me as your mate, I think I clicked with you," he said.

"But we didn't..." She trailed off, blushing.

"Oh, don't think you're getting off that easy," he teased her. "We're definitely going to do that, too."

She smiled and his heart felt like it would expand out of his chest.

"Anyway," he said. "I think you got my gift. Dr. Bhimani said it might happen. And somehow, I think we're making this together."

"Wow," Cecily breathed.

"Yeah," Solo said, looking around. "Wow."

"I always thought the first boy I ever kissed would kiss me right here in the glade," Cecily mused.

"How about if the *last* man you'll ever kiss decided to kiss you here?" Solo asked.

Her eyes danced and she tilted her chin up to him in invitation.

Solo leaned down and kissed her slowly, carefully, reveling in the heat of her sweet mouth, the feel of her hands tightening on his shoulders.

After a moment she pulled away slightly.

"My dad is probably watching us," she whispered.

Solo hadn't thought of that.

"It's time to leave the glade then," he told her.

"How do I do that?" she asked.

"Just reach into your mind and... let go," he explained as best he could.

She closed her eyes.

After a second, the glade faded to the ghostly afterimage he had created himself.

She opened her eyes.

"Oh wow," she said.

"Can you still see it?" he asked her. That had never happened before. Only Solo could see his visions.

"I can see both now," she told him. "The outline of the glade and the actual parking lot."

"You're seeing my vision," he mused.

"No more private visions for you," she teased.

He smiled, closed his eyes, and let go of the glade.

As soon as he opened his eyes he could feel the rain on his head again. Thunder boomed overhead, not so distant this time.

"Hey kids," Dirk Malcolm called from where he stood, leaning on his car with a fond smile on his face. "Want to get out of here before we all get washed away?"

"Absolutely," Cecily replied, taking Solo by the hand and leading him back to the car with her.

"So do you want me to give him a hard time or what?" Dirk asked Cecily. "I'm new to this dad thing, but I'm pretty good at improv. Should I threaten to kill him if he hurts you? Or do I just give him a look that implies I have weapons?"

"He's good, Di... Dad," Cecily said, climbing into the car. "No threats or mean looks needed."

"*She called me Dad,*" Dirk mouthed excitedly to Solo, his eyebrows comically high.

Solo climbed into the car and they headed down the leafy streets of Greenfield.

"You guys are staying at the Greenfield Inn, right?" Dirk

asked. "Or did you want me to help you track down your friends?"

"No," Solo and Cecily said at once.

"Er, no, we'll just go to the hotel," Cecily said. "Would you mind letting my friends know where I am?"

"Sure," Dirk said, looking decidedly uncomfortable.

Solo was grateful that Cecily didn't seem to care.

Rain drummed down on the roof of the car, and the short drive seemed to take forever. But at last they reached the small hotel outside the village, just as the rain began to pour in earnest.

"Thanks for the ride," Cecily said, suddenly sounding awkward.

"Are you kids okay from here?" Dirk asked.

"Sure," she said. "So are you going to the Con in Glacier City?"

"Yeah," he said. "I sure am."

"Would you want to, um, have breakfast or something when we get there?" she asked.

"I would love that." Dirk smiled so hard the lines on his face disappeared.

"Okay, I'll text you," Cecily said, squeezing his knee and hopping out of the car.

Solo hopped out of the back seat and gave Dirk a wave before following Cecily through the deluge to the hotel lobby.

They headed up the stairs quietly to their room on the second floor.

Cecily opened the door and went in. It was a small space with a big bed at its center and a tiny bedside table.

Once Solo closed the door behind them the room seemed small and quiet. There was nothing to distract him from his mate.

Cecily put her bag down on the table and turned to him slowly.

"Are you feeling shy?" he asked her.

She gave him a crooked smile. She was feeling shy.

Her damp t-shirt clung to her curves and raindrops sparkled in her hair like diamonds.

Solo was nearly overwhelmed with the need to pull her close, to warm her body with his and claim her.

"We don't have to consummate our mating tonight," he told her. "We can go find our friends and spend time with them. We have the rest of our lives..."

But she was approaching him slowly, an unmistakable look in her eyes.

"Oh, no," she said. "You're not getting off that easy."

He smiled at how she had turned his words around on him.

And then she was up on her toes, wrapping her arms around his neck and pressing her body to his.

Solo held her gently, enjoying the feel of her cool wet t-shirt and the warm woman beneath it.

Cecily brushed her lips against his. She tasted like rain and hunger.

He kissed her back with all the pent up passion of the last twenty-four hours.

In one rotation of the Earth he had loved and lost and seen her return to his arms again. The emotions were dizzying, and when coupled with the hot demands of his body he felt nearly drunk with relief and desire.

Cecily pressed her breasts against his chest.

Growling, Solo lifted her up and deposited her on the bed.

Cecily giggled and the happy sound sent lightning bolts of need through his veins.

He stripped out of his clothes, loving the way she got quiet again the moment he revealed his muscular torso, and the hungry way her eyes caught on his rigid cock.

"Now you," he said.

She smiled and got up on her knees. Keeping her eyes on his, she peeled her t-shirt up over her head, then unfastened her bra, releasing her beautiful breasts.

Solo's mouth watered at the sight, but Cecily wasn't finished.

She pushed down her waistband, peeling shorts and panties over her hips and off at once.

He fell on her, pressing his body to hers, nearly moaning at the contact with her soft warmth. He kissed her forehead, her eyelids, her cheeks, her chin.

Cecily giggled again, the sound like a symphony, and wrapped her arms around him.

He kissed her sweet lips again, and nuzzled her neck.

She arched her back slightly, inviting.

He brushed his lips against the delicate hollow of her throat, inhaling her light scent, then kissed his way down to her breasts.

Cecily tensed, waiting.

Solo licked one sensitive nipple into his mouth, teasing the other between his thumb and forefinger.

Cecily moaned lightly and arched her back even more.

Solo growled and feasted on her breasts, licking and nipping, and sucking her tender nipples until he felt her hips trembling under him.

She was ready.

He nuzzled her belly and nudged her thighs apart, reveling in her delicate scent.

Cecily tossed her head against the pillow.

Solo smiled. She was more than ready. But he had to taste her first.

He lowered his mouth to her, licked her slowly as she whimpered and trembled.

His own need made him nearly frantic, especially with the taste of her on his lips, but he was determined to go slowly.

Cecily's sex glistened pink and swollen as he lapped and flicked his tongue against her slick opening.

She cried out when he drew a circle around her pouting clitoris with his tongue.

He eased a finger against her, pressing inward until her velvety interior enveloped him, pulsing and throbbing in a way that made him wild to be inside her.

He licked around his fingers and she wiggled and lifted her hips, as if begging for release.

When he was convinced that she couldn't take any more, he nuzzled her inner thigh and pulled back to look at her.

Cecily's curls were spread across the pillow, her eyes hazy with lust, hands gripping the sheets - a wanton angel.

"Are you ready, my love?" he asked her.

"Yes, please," she whispered, lifting her arms to him.

He crawled on top of her and kissed her cheeks, her eyelids, her sweet mouth, as she wrapped her hands around his shoulders.

"I love you," he told her.

He took his cock in his hand and found her tender opening, pressing as gently as he could into that intoxicating warmth.

22

CECILY

Cecily stilled, every cell in her body concentrating on the place where Solo entered her.

He moved so slowly and gently, there was barely any pain in spite of the size of him.

Cecily felt herself pulsing around him, nearly overwhelmed with the pleasant sensation of fullness.

Then he began to move.

Cecily had done this before. But it had never felt like this. Solo wasn't using her body to seek his own release. He was using his body to chase after hers.

Shivers of pleasure went down her spine with every gentle thrust. Solo's low moans told her how much he was restraining his own need.

Cecily felt the tension ratcheting up, filling her like a shaken soda, ready to burst.

She sank her nails into his shoulders, hips lifting helplessly against him. She was racked by the pleasure, stretched so thin by it she had forgotten how to breathe. There were only the rough sounds wrung from him and her own accompanying cries, as Solo plunged inside her again and again, sending her closer and closer to the edge of the cliff but stopping just short of letting her soar into the sky.

"Please," she begged. "Please, please, please..."

He slid a big hand between them and caught her distended clitoris between two fingers and massaged it firmly as he thrust into her again.

Stars swam before Cecily's eyes and then the pleasure was lifting her up, up, up.

She was barely conscious of Solo's rough cries as he swelled impossibly inside her.

They clung to each other helplessly in the throes of their shared climax.

When the last of her tremors had ceased, Solo rolled onto his back, pulling her onto his chest.

She lay there, listening to the slowing beat of his heart as he stroked her back.

"We are one now," he said quietly.

She smiled.

"This makes you happy?" he asked, kissing the top of her head.

"Yeah," she said. "Though a lot of decisions have to be made now."

"Like what?" Solo asked.

"I like my rock and roll lifestyle," Cecily said. "Do we have to settle down?"

"Why would we have to do that?" he asked.

"We didn't use protection just now," she said.

"Protection?"

"Birth control," she said.

"Ah, but I am supposed to have a family," Solo said. "Aerie instructed me to enjoy all aspects of human brotherhood. Do you not want children?"

Cecily thought about it.

"I guess I do," she said. "But I don't want to have to stop doing make-up and special effects to have them."

"Why would you have to stop?" he asked. "Can I not care for our young during our travels?"

Cecily laughed. "You know, I think you'd be good at that."

"Of course I would be good at it," Solo said, sounding slightly affronted. "I'm a bio-engineer, and an efficiency expert. Our children will be healthy and extremely well-managed. And of course I will read them many adventure stories. Though they will not need them because they will grow up learning movie stories from their mother's work."

Cecily smiled.

"Is this to your liking?" Solo asked.

"Yes," she said. "I can't believe I'm saying it, but yes. Yes, it all sounds perfect."

"It is perfect," Solo agreed, sealing it with another kiss on the top of her head.

And though the visions of what their future held were spinning in her mind, Cecily found it easy to close her eyes and drift off as her mate stroked her hair.

23
———
CECILY

C ecily bid farewell to the last fan in line at her booth and then threw a "break time" sign over the table.

Solo had already headed over to where Bea and Kate were hosting a panel discussion about their upcoming film.

Glacier City Comic Con was bigger than the last three put together. And for their little group, the news of the upcoming movie made them headliners.

Cecily smiled at the size of the crowd as she approached.

Solo, Kirk and Buck were watching from the back of the room. Solo waved to her and she hurried over to join them.

On the platform, Bea, Kate and Dirk were sitting behind a table along with a moderator.

"How did you get involved in the project?" the moderator was asking Dirk.

"I really liked the graphic novel," Dirk said. "Bea's vision for this film is amazing. And of course working on the movie will allow me to spend more time with my daughter. I don't know if any of you are familiar with the special effects work of Cecily Page, but she's a phenomenal talent."

Before Cecily's amazed eyes, Dirk slid an iPad out of his bag and held up an image of one of her shifting masks for the audience to see.

Kate had told her that Dirk was constantly showing off her picture and telling everyone who would listen how talented his daughter was, but Cecily hadn't taken it seriously.

Dirk's eyes landed on hers in the audience and he pulled the screen down hurriedly, as if she had caught him with his hand in the cookie jar.

"Anyway," he continued. "There's a lot of fresh talent on this film and I'm glad they'll let an old guy like me take part. I have a feeling I'm going to learn a lot from working with Beatrix Li."

"Beatrix, do you have any parting words for your fans?" the moderator asked.

"Uh, no, but I think Kate does," Bea said.

Kate grinned.

"*Be yourself*," she began.

"*And worlds will follow*," the crowd shouted back.

"Thanks for coming out everyone," the moderator said with a smile.

The crowd dissipated and Cecily and the guys approached the platform.

"How did it go?" she asked Bea.

Bea shrugged coolly, but her eyes were sparkling. Classic Bea.

"It was awesome," Kate said. "Sorry you missed most of it."

"Oh, I saw enough," Cecily said, giving Dirk a look.

He glanced down in a guilty way.

"Hey, Dad, want to go for a little stroll?" she asked.

"That would be great," he said, grabbing his bag and leaping off the platform. "See you guys."

They walked together to the hallway just outside the convention hall.

"Listen, Cecily," Dirk said. "I'm sorry if I'm coming on too strong."

"Hey," she said, sliding her phone out of her pocket and tapping her fingers on the screen for a moment. "There. Check your email."

She watched as he opened the iPad and clicked on her email.

"Password is *aliensummer*, all one word, lowercase," she said.

His eyes widened slightly, but he typed it in.

"I know we missed a lot," Cecily said. "I thought you might want pictures."

She had made him a password-protected webpage with pictures from her childhood. Kate had snagged a box of family photos from the storage locker when they were searching it for clues. Cecily and Solo spent an afternoon at a print shop scanning in the best ones when they arrived in Glacier City.

Then Cecily had set up the page so each one could be captioned to let Dirk know everything she could remember about the day.

There were birthdays, zoo trips, graduations and missing teeth, and even shots of her building sets for the school play.

A few included pictures of her mom. She knew those might hurt Dirk to see, but she had a feeling he would like the memories anyway.

"Cecily," he breathed.

"You can show those to people if you want, or you can

keep them all to yourself," she told him. "But you're part of my life now. So when we add the next birthday picture, I hope you're in it."

Tears streamed down Dirk's cheeks. He crushed Cecily into a bear hug.

"Damn it," he sobbed happily. "I'm supposed to comfort you when *you* cry, kid."

"Hopefully I won't need it," Cecily said. But she hugged him back as hard as she could. It was good having family again.

"Where's that fella of yours?" Dirk asked. "I'll bet he helped you with this. I need to shake his hand."

"He did help me," Cecily said, letting go.

Dirk took her by the hand and they headed back into the convention hall.

Solo was standing with the others, talking with another tall, broad shouldered man who was leaning on a cane as he spoke.

"Well, if you need a venue, I recommend the Glacier City Zoo," he was saying in a deep voice. "I think the board owes my wife a favor."

He turned and left, waving to a curvy lady in a gray pantsuit and pink scarf who stood in the far doorway to the corridor.

"Wait, was that...?" Cecily couldn't finish the question - it was so unlikely.

"Westley Worthington," Beatrix finished it in a shell-shocked way. "In the flesh. He liked my graphic novel. And he was so nice."

"Holy crap," Dirk said, looking after the well-dressed man with the cane.

"Was he suggesting the zoo as a location for us to

shoot?" Cecily asked. It didn't seem like a good location for any scene in the movie.

"No," Bea said slowly, looking down at the ring on her finger.

When Cecily looked up from Bea's finger she saw Solo on his knees in front of her.

"Oh," she managed, her heart pounding in her ears.

"Cecily," Solo said, a slight tremble in his voice. "Will you marry me?"

"Yes," Cecily said immediately. It was easy to say yes, when the man asking the question was already her soul mate.

He held out a slender coppery ring.

"This is made from the penny that was in my pocket the day I met you," he told her as he slipped it onto her finger.

Suddenly a veil dropped over the room and Cecily saw a scene spread before her.

Kate was turning to see the opening bathroom door of the rental they'd shared back in Philadelphia.

She looked shorter than usual.

The door opened all the way to reveal... herself.

It dawned on her that she was seeing it all from Solo's point of view.

She saw the beauty of her curves beneath the towel, the way the droplets of water clung to her hair, the kindness in her own eyes.

And she felt his happy agony of the mate bond, already locking the two of them inexorably together. The weight of it was both honey-sweet and frightening within Solo's chest.

The veil slipped away as Solo slid the ring back off her finger.

"What she doesn't get to keep it?" Kate chided Solo.

He strung it on a chain and offered it to Cecily.

She took it and slid it over her head, then went on her toes to kiss him, long and slow and sweet.

"I love you," he whispered into her hair. "I will follow you everywhere."

"You will never be bored," she whispered back.

"Want to get married at the Glacier City Zoo?" he asked.

"Only if the others will do it too," she said.

"I was hoping you would suggest that," he said. She could hear the smile in his voice.

And though everyone around them began chattering excitedly and her back was being patted in congratulations, Cecily's senses were filled with nothing but her beautiful alien mate.

24

SOLO

S olo stood at the top of the meadow that spanned the space between the elephant enclosure and the wild dog habitat at the Glacier City Zoo.

There was a beautiful view of the sun setting over the water and the buildings of Glacier City glimmering in the distance.

But Solo chose to ignore that view, instead squinting to try and make out whether Cecily and her friends might be coming out of the visitor's center.

He felt no trepidation. The marriage was but a ceremony. Their real bond had been made for him from the moment he had laid eyes on Cecily. In truth from moments even before that, when he had touched the kitchen utensils she had touched before him, and seen a fleeting vision of a woman with flowing ginger ringlets and gentle eyes.

He only felt anxious to have her by his side. This day of preparations and hiding from one another was not to his liking. Besides, the whole thing smacked of inefficiency. It was nonsense that they had arrived here in separate vehicles, not sharing their meals or their lodgings as usual.

To his right, Buck and Kirk waited for their brides as well.

And in the first row of folding chairs more brothers and their mates looked on.

Bond held a small and adorable baby in his arms. Beside him, Posey riffled through her bag, pulling out all kinds of small things that were presumably meant to help care for the tiny creature.

Rocky and his mate, Georgia, shared a kiss in the next set of seats.

Beside them, Rima was talking to Magnum and pointing at the far side of the zoo. Solo wondered if she was explaining the complicated system of levies that held this side of Glacier City afloat - or maybe recounting the tale of how Westley Worthington had sacrificed everything to save this city in the name of his beloved.

Solo longed to examine the blueprints for the system himself, but his new friend West had merely clapped him on the back and told him to get married first and then come for a visit to pour over as many blueprints as he liked.

Solo wondered if he might pursue work as a consultant in what Earth scientists called *civil engineering*. He was fascinated with the challenges of maintaining a city in the face of Earth's vast fluctuations in wind, water and temperature. It reminded him of his own work on Aerie designing ships to withstand the journey of light-years. So long as he could do it from a laptop on the road with Cecily and their children, he felt the work would be a perfect match for his skills.

There was a slight commotion and he looked up to see Kate emerging from the visitor's center.

Her blonde hair was straight down her back and the simple white gown she wore did not distract from her lovely brown eyes, which filled with tears the moment they gazed upon Kirk.

Beatrix came next. She wore a white lace gown with fingerless lace gloves to her elbows. Her hair was swept up on top of her head. A black velvet sash around her waist was an homage to her everyday favorite color.

Beside him, Buck sighed happily when he saw her.

But Solo was already watching the doorway for Cecily.

At last she emerged.

Her coppery curls were loose around her shoulders, matching the wink of the copper ring that hung from the delicate chain around her neck. The pale cream satin gown she wore was beautiful against her milky complexion.

She walked toward him with a quiet confidence, a solemn expression on her beautiful face.

Solo thought his chest might rupture with joy.

A soft trumpeting sound came from the second row of seats.

Solo looked down to see Dirk Malcolm blowing his nose while Aunt Stacy patted his back.

He glanced back at Cecily, who grinned and rolled her eyes slightly.

Laughter bubbled in his chest, and suddenly this was just another wonderful adventure with his mate.

The words of the ceremony went quickly. Solo managed to remember his part.

And when it was all over and he was permitted to kiss his bride, he made sure to go slow and sweet so that it would be a kiss she could remember forever.

Then suddenly music was playing and Beatrix had kicked off her shoes and begun to dance, her hair already coming out of its bun as Buck laughed and tried to keep up.

Kate and Kirk danced in each other's arms. Though Solo

was certain the tempo of the music was not proper for that kind of dance, he was glad that the two of them appeared to be more than content.

"Now what?" he asked his mate. "Do you want to dance?"

Cecily gazed out at the crowd of their friends looking happy but ponderous.

"I just want to remember it," she said at last. "Things change in time, but for right now we're all together, and everything seems to be perfect."

Solo slipped the rose out of his top jacket button.

"You can replay it again as many times as we like," he told her, holding out the bloom. "I've been holding onto this all day. It should be practically overflowing with memories by now."

She smiled, like sunshine after a rain.

"Do you have time for a picture with your old man?" Dirk asked, jogging up to them.

"Sure we do," Cecily said, looking up at Solo, her eyes dancing. "We have all the time in the world."

***

Thanks for reading Solo!
Keep reading for a sample of the next Stargazer Alien Mail Order Brides book: Drago.

Or grab your next book right now:
http://www.tashablack.com/stargazer.html

DRAGO (SAMPLE)

1

ARDEN

Arden Green was dreaming of peach trees.

In the dream, she was trespassing again.

Most days she managed to keep her head down in the lab. She documented every conceivable action of her charges from sun up to sundown with quick breaks for lunch and dinner.

But now and again the endless indoor routine got the best of her and instead of eating her lunch she slipped out the back, across the field and past the rhododendron hedge to the farm on the other side of the lab.

It was no surprise that was where her dream had taken her.

Arden peered around the hedge.

Just as when she visited in her waking hours, there was no sign of life on the other side. Not only in the orchard - there were no sounds of people or machinery coming from the rest of the farm either. Arden sometimes wondered how a farm could be run with so little activity.

But for today, she was grateful for the opportunity to convene with nature for a moment.

She stepped into the orchard. The air was rich with the scent of dewy grass and loamy soil.

The wildly gnarled branches of the trees overhead were at odds with their prim, perfectly spaced rows. Feathery green leaves trembled lightly in the breeze.

Prunis persica - the common peach tree. It was not native to North America. Like the men Arden cared for and studied, it had been transported from far, far away.

Arden lifted her hands and let the leaves tickle her palms as she walked between two of the rows.

Feel the sun on your face, taste the summer in the air.

These things are timeless pleasures.

Compared with them, Drago is a passing thought.

But when she closed her eyes to soak in the sunlight, it was his fingers caressing her hands, his smile warming her face.

Suddenly she was aware of the breeze against her skin.

In the dream, she opened her eyes.

And Drago was there.

He stood just down the row of trees from Arden, his hands outstretched to mirror hers. Sunlight glinted golden in his hair.

Arden gasped.

He wasn't supposed to be out of the lab.

Drago's blue eyes blazed into hers as he took a deliberate step forward, and then another.

Arden froze, waiting for him. Her heart pounded as if she had just run a marathon.

They were alone. She had never been alone with him.

He moved faster now, his jaw rippled with tension as if he were angry.

But Arden knew better. She could feel the sizzle of lust that hummed in the shrinking space between them.

Her own body ached in sympathy. She needed him too. Burned for him to wrap his arms around her, tear off the clothing that separated them, and possess her in the way they both had wanted since the first time their eyes met.

He stopped just in front of her.

Arden gazed up at him, pleading mutely.

Drago pressed his palms to hers.

Something powerful passed between them, a current that electrified her blood and made her bold.

Arden went up on her toes to kiss him.

There was a sound in the air, as if the breeze had strengthened and was sending the leaves of the peach trees into frenzied applause.

But Drago brought his mouth down to claim hers and Arden forgot everything but the warmth of his mouth and the feel of his hard body pressing against her softness.

She pressed back, stifling a moan.

Drago cupped her cheek with one big hand and gripped her hip with the other, as if he were afraid she would try to get away.

She kissed him back, drunk on the taste of his mouth, the feel of his big body in her arms at last.

He broke the kiss to gaze down at her.

"Arden," he whispered, his eyes tender now instead of fierce. "Arden."

She opened her mouth to reply, but something was wrong, she couldn't speak.

"Arden," Dr. Bhimani's voice crackled as it came through the intercom.

Arden blinked and the orchard faded away.

She was back in her bunk, tangled in the sheets, dreaming about one of the men she'd been brought there to observe.

"Yes, Dr. Bhimani," she replied, hoping her voice didn't give away that she wasn't fully awake yet.

"Sorry to disturb you," Dr. Bhimani said. "I wondered if you might be able to visit me today during your dinner break."

"Of-of course," Arden stammered, hoping she wasn't in trouble.

"Thank you so much, Arden," Dr. Bhimani said. "See you at the lab."

There was a crackle and the intercom went silent.

Arden grabbed her phone. It was still early, but she might as well get up. After all, she certainly wasn't going to be able to sleep again.

She headed for the showers, grateful no one else was around.

Most of the lab techs left for the weekends, so Arden and two of the male techs were the only ones around. She got some extra pay, and she had no place to go over the weekend anyway. Her family was all out west, in the suburbs of Glacier City.

Once she was showered and dressed, Arden felt more like herself. She buttoned a fresh lab coat over her clothing and pulled her hair back in its usual ponytail.

She walked across the field to the lab, trying to ignore the scent of peaches in the air. It was just the fragrance in the shampoo she'd bought at the grocery store in town, not real peaches. It was too early in the season for there to be any fruit on the trees yet. The shampoo was likely the reason she'd dreamt of the peach orchard next door in the first place.

"Hey, Arden," one of the male techs said as she walked in.

"Hey, Tom," she replied.

She could tell by the sounds in the lab that the first session of the morning had started early. Tom held an empty box in his hands, and their colleague, Russ, was already halfway down his row.

"You got an early start, huh?" Arden asked.

"We're going into Philly tonight," Tom said, waggling his eyebrows. "Hitting the Stackhouse. You want in?"

"No thanks," Arden wrinkled her nose.

She had no interest in spending her free time, or her meager stipend, at some casino. Knowing how much they made, she doubted Tom could really afford to be a high roller either. But she supposed everyone needed to blow off a little steam from time to time.

"Suit yourself," Tom shrugged.

Arden grabbed her own box of VHS tapes from the shelf at the end of the lab.

The titles popped out at her garishly.

Frontin' the Booty

Flashpoint X

A Clockwork Orgy

Much as she tried to view her job as scientific, some parts of it were easier than others.

She made her way to the first booth and tapped on the frame.

The curtain moved aside and a masculine face greeted her.

"Good morning, Arden," the man said.

He was as stunning as an underwear model, and wearing nothing but a terrycloth robe. But he had an innocence about him that made things a little easier.

"Hello," Arden replied. She wasn't supposed to make small talk at this point in the experiment.

She stepped into the booth and put a tape into the small

TV/VCR combo that was the only thing in the booth besides the man, a plastic specimen cup, and a container of wipes.

"You know what to do," she said.

He nodded, his hands already eagerly tugging at the sash of the robe.

She moved on to the next booth, and the next.

Sounds of pleasure were echoing through the laboratory, the keens and cries of a hundred porn stars begging for five hundred movie orgasms.

On her first day Arden had been red in the face and convinced she would quit by lunchtime. She couldn't really be expected to hand out porn to a bunch of men like she was slinging burgers at a diner.

But these weren't really men.

They were visitors from the planet Aerie.

At home, the citizens of Aerie were gaseous forms, floating among the crags and living on starlight.

But they had received welcoming transmissions from Earth in the 1980s, transmissions that were sent from the observatory next to the lab, right here in Stargazer, Pennsylvania.

After studying the movies and culture of the planet during that era, the scientists of Aerie had designed human bodies and transported the men into them so that they might visit their Earthly friends.

And they had designed those human bodies very carefully.

Each man's form was perfectly crafted to inspire lust in the women of Earth. Each of them seemed to be taller and more muscular than the last.

Once they arrived, if the men *clicked* into the human forms they became human forever.

So far, the only way to do that seemed to be through the

mating bond. The first three aliens to arrive had come in secret, and had been allowed to interact with human women outside the lab. They had fallen in love and each had *clicked* when he bonded to his mate.

Now Earth's government and Aerie's wanted to know if it could be accomplished without relying on something as unpredictable as love.

So Arden's job was simple.

She helped the aliens try to *click* on their own, using nothing but good old-fashioned pornography.

At first they had used modern porn, but the men had been overwhelmed by what they saw. When Dr. Bhimani sent Tom to the old video store in town for VHS tapes they had turned a corner. Now these 80s and 90s movies were the soundtrack to Arden's mornings and evenings.

She had grown used to it - as used to it as she could be.

Except when it came to the last booth in her row.

She approached it now, tapping timidly on the frame.

The curtain opened slowly.

Drago gave her a slow smile.

Something swarmed in her chest, like butterflies made of fire.

"Good morning, Arden Green," Drago said, his blue eyes glittering dangerously. Somehow, this one lacked the innocence of his brothers.

"Good morning," she said quickly, grabbing a tape at random from her box.

Drago chuckled.

She looked down at the cassette in her hand.

Weird Science XXX: Starring Kelly LeKnockers

The cover showed a woman with long brown hair in a ponytail and a lab coat. She looked oddly similar to Arden - except that Kelly LeKnockers's lab coat was unbuttoned to reveal a pair of enormous bare breasts. A big blond man knelt at her feet, hands outstretched as if to touch them.

Horrified, but too embarrassed to back out, Arden leaned forward to insert the tape into the VCR.

Instead, she dropped it on the floor at Drago's feet.

***

Thanks for reading this sample of Drago!
Grab the rest of the story now:
http://www.tashablack.com/stargazer.html

TASHA BLACK STARTER LIBRARY

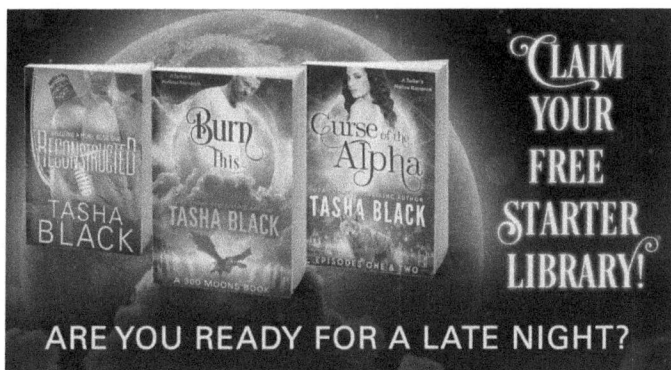

Packed with steamy shifters, mischievous magic, billionaire superheroes, and plenty of HEAT, the Tasha Black Starter Library is the perfect way to dive into Tasha's unique brand of Romance with Bite!

Get your FREE books now at tashablack.com!

ABOUT THE AUTHOR

Tasha Black lives in a big old Victorian in a tiny college town. She loves reading anything she can get her hands on, writing paranormal romance, and sipping pumpkin spice lattes.

Get all the latest info, and claim your FREE Tasha Black Starter Library at www.TashaBlack.com

Plus you'll get the chance for sneak peeks of upcoming titles and other cool stuff!

Keep in touch...
www.tashablack.com
authortashablack@gmail.com

facebook.com/romancewithbite
twitter.com/romancewithbite

Lightning Source UK Ltd.
Milton Keynes UK
UKHW04f1854081018
330211UK00001B/18/P

9 781723 376641